STOLEN OATH

MAYA DANIELS

Vinci Books

vinci-books.com

Published by Vinci Books Ltd in 2026

1

Copyright © Maya Daniels 2023

The author has asserted their moral right to be identified as the author of this work in accordance with the Copyright, Designs and Patents Act 1988. This work is a work of fiction. Names, characters, places and incidents are the product of the author's imagination or are used fictitiously. Any resemblance to actual persons, living or dead, places and incidents is entirely coincidental.
All rights reserved. No part of this publication may be copied, reproduced, distributed, stored in any retrieval system, or transmitted in any form or by any means, including photocopying, recording, or other electronic or mechanical methods, nor used as a source for any form of machine learning including AI datasets, without the prior written permission of the publisher.
The publisher and the author have made every effort to obtain permissions for any third party material used in this book and to comply with copyright law. Any queries in this respect should be brought to the attention of the publisher and any omissions will be corrected in future editions.
A CIP catalogue record for this book is available from the British Library.
Paperback ISBN: 9781036705879
The EU GPSR authorised representative is Logos Europe, 9 rue Nicolas Poussion, 17000 La Rochelle, France contact@logoseurope.eu

By Maya Daniels

Honor Among Thieves
Stolen Magic
Stolen Oath

Infernal Regions for the Unprepared
Black Hand
Lower World
Everlasting Fire
Place of Torment
Hellfire to Come

The Broken Halos Series
The Devil is in the Details
Speak of the devil
Encounter with the Devil
The Devil in Disguise
To Look the Devil in the Eye
Better the Devil You Know
Give a Devil his Due

Daywalker series
Investigated
Infiltrated
Instigated
Initiated

Infuriated

Ignited

Chronicles of Forbbiden Witchery

Resting Witch Face

Pitch a Witch

Witch Please

Payback is a Witch

The Necronomicon Guardian series

The Magician

The High Priestess

The Courtless Fae Series

Secret Origins

Hidden Portals Trilogy

Venus Trap

The First Secret

The Last Note

Sound

Sonata

By Maya Daniels

The Cursed Kingdom

Chapter One

The cheery chime of the bell above the door registered at the back of my subconscious like an annoyingly persistent buzzing of a mosquito. It echoed perpetually behind my eyeballs to the point of madness. Being agitated made me twitchy and unreasonable at the best of times, so you could imagine my state of mind that morning.

A jerk was an understatement of what I was.

My brain was mush from the lack of sleep in the last couple of weeks, and naturally, any type of noise didn't help much in my attempts to stay sane or civil. I wanted to snarl and snap at anyone who walked into the store just to make sure every single person was as miserable as I was.

Adulting at its finest, I had no doubt.

The truth of the matter is, I wanted to be numb and to be grateful for the numbness; Because then I wouldn't have to acknowledge the crushing weight of my guilt while suffocating under it. I neither knew, nor cared, I just wanted the weight of the elephant sitting on my chest gone.

Thinking myself invincible, I stole a magic book full of

ancestral spells—that was not supposed to exist, mind you—from none other than Dimitri Bell, alpha of the Southern California pack and newest member of the MPO.

My ego, as I always feared, would be my downfall.

The fact that it was Dimitri's father who hired me sent all of us into an impossible situation between a rock and a hard place. Instead of coming up with a solid plan, the old alpha pushed us into a corner where we acted rashly and defensively, and because of that, my best friend dabbled in blood magic and potions that were best left alone for goodness sake. As a result, she lost part of herself in the process.

I wanted to shriek and rage until I destroyed myself and there was nothing left of me.

I failed Char, I failed Dimitri, and I failed myself too. And for what?

Nothing. That's what.

Others were paying for my mistakes.

Char was paying for them more than anyone else, which was the core of my problem if I is being honest.

A ray of sunshine was caught in a slow, sensual dance with one of the crystals, casting bursts of colors across the floor like a liquid fire snaking over the vinyl before it bounced up and glittered over the displayed candles and statues. The coward that I am, I watched it with a desperation of a man dying from thirst seeing a fat, juicy droplet of water. It was going great too until someone cleared their throat close enough that I could smell the tuna this person has eaten in the last hour or so for breakfast.

"Welcome to the Crystal Palace," I mumbled dully and dragged my eyes from the floor to the person in front of the counter. "How can I help you?"

"Namaste." The young woman smiled demurely at me before bowing her head in a practiced swan move she must've done at least a thousand times in front of a mirror. How I knew? It was either practiced or she was a time traveler from the Middle Ages where she curtsied and bowed to royalties and suitors on a daily basis. She was all elegance and grace that was faker than the three-inch caterpillar lashes the lady checking out the incense to our right had glued to her poor eyelids.

I glanced briefly at the paperweight sitting inconspicuously next to the register and felt guilty about it immediately. Guilty that I caught myself eyeing it, and for wanting to throw it at swan lake in front of me. Instead of doing what I wanted to do, I forced a smile and jerked my head in a nod.

"Namaste to you too. What can I do for you?"

"I was hoping to find one of the love candles you normally have displayed in that corner." Her arm lifted gracefully as she pointed toward the left corner of the store where the specialty candles were lined up like soldiers. An empty space gapped in the spot where a red love candle usually sat.

"I'm sorry, I didn't notice we sold the last one. I can make one for you but you'll have to come back and pick it up later this afternoon or tomorrow. Whatever works for you, as long as you leave a deposit." My hand was already reaching for the register so I can charge her and get her away from me as fast as I could, but it wasn't written in the stars it seemed.

"But I need it now." With a sharp, reprimanding voice, she folded her arms over her chest and my hand froze a hairsbreadth away from the register. "Not later this afternoon and not tomorrow, that's for sure. Now, sister." The last part was said almost mockingly. I knew I should've stayed home and avoided any interaction.

Something primal and scary perked up inside of me at her tone, and like the predator that I was, my head cocked to the side on its own and my vision sharpened on her features. For the first time, I noticed the tiny beads of sweat around her hairline and on her upper lip, which was trembling slightly despite her holier-than-thou attitude.

My instincts were screaming at me that something was off about the lady.

"And why is that, sister?" Not even my sneer made her pay attention that she was treading on dangerous grounds. "What's so important that can't wait a few hours? We don't sell generic, mass-market candles. Each is made here in the shop."

"You don't understand and I don't expect you to, but I can't stand a second longer with her having those painted claws all over him. He needs to come back to where he belongs. With me. Now, not this afternoon or tomorrow." With each word she was becoming more agitated and she tapped her forefinger on the counter to make her point.

"You're looking for a candle to return a lost lover?" My eyes narrowed suspiciously on her.

It wasn't my place to question customers. For my morals' sake, I wanted to occasionally, maybe, but not if I wanted to run a successful business. After all, I prided myself that I did something good with the candles, even when everything else in my life was pushing the limits of ethical grounds. Yet memories of Dimitri and the desperation in his eyes when he talked about his obligations along with placating his father in hopes to keep him away from destroying his life raked my insides with razor blades. The fact that I would've felt better if the handsome alpha was unattached had nothing to do with it. I almost convinced myself of that too.

Almost.

"We were happy." A tear glistened in her right eye that rolled down her cheek and I tracked every twitch of her muscles like a hawk. "I was his world until she came along and convinced him they were soulmates. She must've given him a potion or something. I need him back."

"Because he is your soulmate? Not hers?"

The shop disappeared into a blurry fog when I focused solely on her, and in slow motion I watched her chest expand as she took a deep breath while another tear rolled down her face. My problem was, the sadness which usually pulled at my heartstrings as customers asked for my aid was missing from her hooded gaze. Instead, rage lurked in her irises, calling to the magic inside my veins to come to the surface and burn everything in my path. My intuition reacted to her deceit immediately.

"Yes." The young woman lifted her hand and casually tucked a strand of strawberry blonde hair behind her ear. The bracelets on her forearm slid down and tinkled in the silence that hummed in my ears. "Mine. Not hers."

And there it was, that cunning glint in her eyes. If I wasn't watching her as closely as I was, I would've missed it.

"You don't need a love candle for that." Leaning back casually so she doesn't notice I was trying to distance myself from whatever was off with her, I gave her a practiced smile. "I have something better. Wait right here."

Her face cleared and the sadness she faked horribly was replaced by triumph, instantly.

Should I have kept my nose out of her business? Probably.

Was it my job to teach her a lesson? Absolutely not.

Was I going to stick my nose in her business and teach

her a lesson she will never forget nonetheless? Hell yeah, I was.

You don't get to play with people's lives and get away with it.

Not if I can help it.

My flats whispered over the tiled floor as I rushed to the back of the store where my candles waited their turn to be displayed. Not wasting time, in case I changed my mind, I practically snatched the multicolored one from the top of the box it was perched on. The patterned texture of the purple wax rasped over my fingers almost in a loving caress when the traces of my magic I'd left in it reacted to my presence. I glanced down at it, checking that the black and red inside layers were a perfect thickness out of habit and my thumb rubbed the black tourmaline stone pressed on the outside layer at the center, making sure it won't wobble or dislodge. It wont do any good if the stone is not on the candle when it does the reverse spell it was meant to do.

The curtain grazed the exposed skin on my back where the tank top didn't cover it when I returned to the front of the store and I shivered. Another chill crawled up my spine at the voracious look the woman had while her eyes were glued to my hand holding the beautiful candle.

A small tug curled one side of my mouth at her expression.

"What is it for?" she breathed out in anticipation, already reaching outward with her greedy fingers so she can touch the candle.

"This one will restore everything the way it was," I said proudly and truthfully. "No need for rituals, full moon, or chanting. Just go home, light it up, and say thank you."

Without looking away from it, she waved her credit card at me and snatched the candle hard enough to leave wax under my fingernails because I didn't release it fast enough. A sensation I couldn't name poked its head up inside me but I pushed it away. There were more important things to deal with than horrible humans like the one impatiently waiting on me to finish the transaction.

So engrossed in my thoughts, I didn't notice we were not alone at the register anymore. My heart skipped a beat when I lifted my head to hand her her card with the receipt and a storm blue gaze captured mine like a snare.

"Thank you so much, sister." The woman yanked her card from my fingers but I couldn't look at her if I tried. Instead, I blinked at the person standing behind her. "Namaste," she spat at me, and then she was gone.

"Let me guess, that was not a love candle?" Dimitri glided closer and casually leaned on the counter. The scent of citrus and musk tickled my nose and my belly tightened in reaction to his nearness sending butterflies into a frenzy in my lower belly.

"How long were you standing there?" I had to clear my throat because I sounded breathless to the point of embarrassment and ducked my head so I could hide my face with my hair.

"Long enough to know that poor guy is not her soulmate?" He murmured the statement more like a question and his eyebrow cocked up as he side-eyed me. Transixed I peaked at him through the strands of hair covering half of my face. "Or that the candle she bought is not a love candle." A small smile played on his lips. He spoke as if he was reprimanding me, yet he never said anything of the sort, remaining quiet and watching the woman walk out of the store with the candle.

"You trust my judgment?" It's not like I wanted his

approval or anything, but my tone suggested that I very much did.

"To a point, yes. I trust this too." He tapped his nose with his forefinger and a braided, leather cord dangled from his wrist that hit me like a punch to the gut. "I can smell a lie from a mile away." Wolves gave each other promised leather cords to wear on their wrists when they were engaged. My jaw clenched tight enough to grind my molars and of course the alpha didn't miss my reaction. I was grateful he chose to let it slide since I've already embarrassed myself in front of him more times than I'd like to count. "What does the candle do?" He searched my face while I composed myself to answer him without squeaking like a five-year-old.

"It restores the balance. Everything she has done to tweak anyone's mind or actions, or any negative energy she sent out will return to her… tenfold." My shoulder twitched in a half shrug like it was nothing, though it was anything but. "I hope she shopped elsewhere for anything she's done until today. It'll be horrible to know I've unintentionally helped her do bad things to people if she has been buying her tools in my store."

"Vicious, Miss McCullough." The grin brightened his face so much it made it look almost boyish.

Yet there was nothing boyish at all about Dimitri Bell.

"I don't like it when someone tries to mess with people and their free will." My tone was sharp and short, maybe even a tid bit louder than intended. I found myself defensive for some silly reason. "People should not be forced to do anything they choose not to do. Not if I can help it, anyway." *You shouldn't do anything against your will either,-* but that part I kept to myself.

Dimitri sharpened his gaze on me and stayed silent long

enough to make me want to squirm where I stood. I resisted with everything in me and watched fascinated as something clicked behind his stormy irises as he either made a decision or I confirmed something for him. Whatever it was, I truly believe that very moment, for better or for worse, sealed both our fates.

"I hope you hold that word. As a matter of fact, I'm counting on it, Allie." He said my nickname with a barely there rasp to his tone, which made me tremble visibly. To add insult to injury, he winked after seeing the effect he had on me.

In answer, my snort had no humor in it, yet he threw his head back and laughed as if I had told him the funniest joke ever.

I did say he was a jerk, didn't I?

Chapter Two

"Why are you here again?" Pretending I was busy, and failing miserably, I kept rearranging the crystals over and over so I don't have to maintain eye contact with Dimitri. Or keep thinking about the woman and her lies.

His wolf unnerved me on the best of days. Why was he in my store? Why?

"I thought friends visit each other?" Reaching over my shoulder and standing too close for comfort, he nudged a crustal to the right unnecessarily. My attempt to get away from him was unsuccessful. He just followed leisurely behind me no matter where I went. "Was I wrong in my assumption? You look upset that I am here. Why?"

That thick accent of his was to blame for my knees being wobbly. He knew exactly what he was doing and stupidly, I did nothing to stop him. I didn't smack his hand when his fingers grazed my arm as he stepped back either. I simply shivered like a fool. Witch or not, I was a woman, damn it.

I was weak when it came to Dimitri Bell.

"We're friends now?" My mouth snapped shut as soon as the words were out. It shouldn't have sounded like a challenge but it did. His low chuckle confirmed my stupidity.

"What would you like us to be if not friends, Miss McCullough?" Dimitri slid close enough that I could feel the heat of his body on my skin. Without a conscious thought, my body leaned back to be closer to him before I became aware of my actions. When I did become aware of what I was doing I jerked away from him as if electricted.

"We should ask your fiancée," I ground out between my teeth. "I'm sure she would love to tell us the answer."

A statue rattled on a shelf nearby, snapping me out of the fog my brain dived into around the alpha. The lady who bumped it grimaced while her face reddened, as if she felt bad for getting my attention while eavesdropping on our conversation. One look around and I realized that the store had filled up while I was too busy swooning at Dimitri like a school girl, and everyone was watching us, watching him to be exact, while pretending they were busy perusing the merchandize. It was like a bucket of cold water being dumped over my head. Feeling sick to my stomach from my beheivor I straightened my shoulders, jutting my chin out stubbornly. I was the master of my emotions not the other way around.

Dimitri had the same effect on any breathing creature. Male or female alike.

He was a juicy steak in the center of a group of hungry beasts.

"I'm an idiot." Angrily smacking his hand away from where he was curling a strand of my hair around his finger, I practically ran for the register. Salvation waited for me as soon as I placed the glass display between us, at least, I hoped that it would. "I don't want us to be anything, Mr. Bell. I do, however, want you to leave my store, if you don't mind. I have things to do instead of playing these games with you."

"I'm not sure how it's good for business to chase away customers." Goddess help me, unperturbed, he stalked me inside my own store. The nerve of this guy.

"You're a customer now?" I tripped while diving behind the register and whacked my elbow on the edge of the counter. My eyes rolled to the back of my head from the stabbing pain that radiated up and down my arm, numbing it all the way to my shoulder. I thought I heard a tooth crack from how hard I clenched my jaw so I wouldn't yelp.

"Of course, I'm a customer," Dimitri said simply and, without permission, reached over the counter, pulled my arm across it, and leaned over to inspect the red, rapidly swelling spot marking my injury. "Supporting local, small businesses is very important for the economy."

Lips parted, I gawked at the top of his head while he gently lifted my arm and soothed my pain by blowing air on it. Gripping the counter in a white-knuckled desperation prevented my fingers from sinking into his hair. My chest tightened because the simple act overwhelmed me with an emotion I didn't dare name. Goose bumps puckered along my skin from the heat that radiated from his pursed lips.

I was in so much trouble.

"How very benevolent of you." My barely above a whisper comment made him glance up at me and my heart skipped a beat from his penetrating stare. "But honestly, I thought we agreed to meet up only when necessary to avoid complications. We can't afford to mess up and trigger some of your father's memories. Not when Char already paid a steep price for it. We're not ready to face him or anyone else that might be involved until we find out more about this whole thing."

"You will forgive me, Alaska, but I cannot sit and pretend like everything is normal, or whatever passes for normal these days for any of us. We know there is more to the situation than just my father wanting to remove me from a position of power or to expose you for... well, you know." Ignoring the hungry looks the women were throwing his way, he rubbed his thumb over the sore spot on my arm, slightly frowning at it, while I frantically searched the store to make sure no one could hear him. The fear for my life made me forget he was touching me like he had every right to do so. I needn't worry though, because he seemed like he was talking more to himself than me and I just happened to be near enough to hear him. "If that was the endgame, he could've gotten me killed or you captured. I need to do something. Anything."

"He can try to catch me anytime he wants." My arrogant snort told him exactly what I thought the chances of anyone catching me were. Well, anyone but Dimitri. As far as I knew, there were no other witches in LA. "Let's hope he holds his breath for it, it might save us all a lot of trouble if he kicks the bucket from oxygen deprivation, but it's not from lack of trying to kill you on his part that you are still alive, wolf. Did you forget the images?" A shiver worked its way up my body when the memory of being underwater while the ocean raged around me squeezed me in its grip.

It also brought another thing to the forefront of my mind. The fact that in my panic, while thinking we were about to die, I stole magic from the elementals and rendered them human, petrified me.

"No." Lifting his gaze to mine, he held me suspended in

a space where the oxygen was thinning with each beat of my heart. "How can I forget that you saved my life, *lyubimyy milyy*."

"Yeah…" Breathless and bothered like every time he would say something in Russian and I had no doubt it was another endearment as was his style, I shook my head to clear it. "I'm dumb like that." My mind told me to take a step back and put more distance between us but I couldn't move to save my life. My feet were glued to the floor.

"And here I thought you cared." He clicked his tongue in faked disappointment before removing his hand from my injured elbow, taking away with him the tantalizing scent that was clouding my mind, and straightening to his full height. Without the physical connection, I finally felt like I could breathe again, though I hated that I missed his touch almost immediately.

"What does it mean?" I asked, despite the fact I knew it was a bad idea. "What you just called me."

He simply smiled, not giving me an answer.

"There was an unexpected development recently in regards to our arrangement. I was hoping to speak with you,"—the shifter looked around the store for the first time and appeared surprised to see it was almost packed. Little did he know, it had nothing to do with the merchandise I was selling and everything to do with the handsome male in front of me—"privately. Let me take you to lunch."

"You could've just called if you wanted to ask me to lunch," I grumbled petulantly, glancing pointedly at the phone perched close to the register in a not so subtle way of telling him *don't you dare call my cell phone*. That'd be a little too familiar for my peace of mind. "Sorry, but it's too early for lunch, plus I'm alone this morning. I can't go anywhere until Char comes to work."

There. That was a good excuse to avoid temptation.

"Speaking of which…" Dimitri smiled as he watched the front door suddenly and expectantly.

The bell above the door rattled a second later, filling the space with the annoyingly cheery chime. Damn shifters and their supernatural hearing. I bet he heard my best friend walking this way from a mile away. The widening of his grin when he looked back at me confirmed it while I glared daggers at his smug face.

"Brunch then." He had the gall to wink, again.

"You can bow now, peasant, your goddess is here." Char swooped in with a grace of a falcon, zeroing in on me from across the store, and saved Dimitri from a nasty curse. I had a couple of them circling in my mind that would've made him regret being all cocky.

Not that I would've cursed him for real. It was just a better alternative to think about that than imagining all the ways I would've loved to climb him like a tree.

A few chuckles met Char's theatrical entrance, the regulars being familiar with our typical antics, and they either waved at her or simply sent her kisses. Everyone loved Char. The moment my bestie locked eyes with me though, I knew something was wrong and my back stiffened.

"I hold your life in my hand." To hide her emotions, she made a show of lifting the paper tray full of coffee cups like it was the holy grail, but I could read the uneasiness she felt in every muscle of her body.

Unsure of what was going on I played along, grabbing at the air in the direction of the coffee she bought for us. "Gimme. I could kiss you right now for bringing a couple of extra cups."

"Pfft, who in their right mind would be happy with just one cup? I can tease men by batting my eyelashes without giving them my phone number. I don't have a death wish to tease a woman with just one cup of coffee." Char proceeded to bat her lashes at Dimitri who in turn, snickered.

"Miss Marietti, it is a pleasure to see you again." Dimitri took hold of Char's shoulders in his hands and kissed her once on each cheek.

"Dimitri!" You'd think the two of them were best friends since birth with how my best friend beamed at him. I was biting the inside of my cheek so I that couldn't tell them where to shove it. They'd been acting like this the last week or so. "*Kak tvoy osel?*" she spoke slowly and deliberately in his mother tongue, vibrating from excitement.

Char can speak Russian? Say what now?

Dimitri threw his had back and laughed heartedly.

"Oh, dear goddess." Char slapped her free hand over her mouth and giggled. "Please tell me I didn't insult your mother?"

I gawked at them.

"You did not." Shoulders still shaking from laughter, he took the tray of coffee cups from her hand and placed it on the counter. "And to answer your question, if I had a donkey, I assure you it would be doing amazingly well. I, on the other hand, am very hungry, but Miss McCullough here refuses to take me to lunch."

"I asked how your donkey is doing?" Char shook her head, laughing along with him. "This will teach me to blindly trust the internet." Curls bouncing, she turned to me, with a raised brow and a smirk on her beautiful face. "And you, Missy? Why are you keeping the wolf hungry? You hoping he will give up on food and gobble you up?"

I felt the heat on my face bloom like a cloud around my

head. Dimitri was snickering along with her but his smoldering gaze added a few extra degrees to the temperature of my reddening cheeks. It was up to me to put a stop to their nonsense.

"What's wrong?" I searched Char's face, ignoring the alpha who was watching me as if he was trying to memorize my features. A maddening hum was thudding in my ears as my heart sped up from his attention.

Glancing left and right to assure no one was near, my best friend leaned in toward me. "I think someone has been following me all morning. That's why it took me so long to get here. I tried to lose whoever it was."

All humor forgotten, Dimitri and I sobered up immediately. My skin prickled from the power that the alpha unleashed, warning anything supernatural within a ten-mile radius that this was his territory and that he will protect it at all costs.

I've heard stories about alphas of his caliber, I'd just never experienced it at that level. He was terrifying in that moment as much as he was exuberant. Primal.

"Mages?" Keeping my tone low, I reached under the counter and pulled out the two kukri knives I stashed there for emergency situations after the vampire attack in our apartment not long ago. Their weight in my palms grounded me to the present more than anything else could've.

"I'm not sure." Char's dark eyes sparkled with anger as she leaned in even closer. "Humans were everywhere this morning so I couldn't do anything about it, but if the stalkers step foot in here, it's game on." Pulling away from me with a wicked and humorless smile, she patted her purse. "I'm going to split them up."

A shiver worked its way up my spine. I loved her to pieces but she scared the crap out of me sometimes.

Suddenly, the bell above the door rattled, filling the store with a jolly peal. All three of our heads snapped toward the entrance, our bodies tensed up and ready to go.

"It's them," Char breathed out.

Chapter Three

Two bulky figures appeared at the entrance of the store looking ominous in their tactical attire while the blindingly bright sun behind them hid their faces from us. All I could notice were the blonde strands of hair appearing almost golden on one of them, while the other obviously had darker colored mop on top of his head. I blinked a few times, hoping to clear my vision so that I can see them better as if that would tell me what they were. Instead, they appeared like faceless shadows to my eyes. Too bad for them though that they couldn't hide their true nature from Dimitri, or more specifically, his sniffer.

Lifting my own nose slightly up in the air, I subtly inhaled in hopes to get some info on our assailants. No ozone scent filled the store and I exhaled in a rush. They were not mages, and since it was not yet noon, not vampires either. A crazy thought crossed my mind that maybe we can talk it out and send the two uninvited supernaturals on their way.

As if reading my mind, a low growl started in the

alpha's chest, vibrating the air around him. Luckily for the humans they couldn't feel magic. I was not that foryunate. It resonated inside my sternum so strongly that you'd think we were connected by a cord. For some unexplainable reason, I could've sworn the anger bubbling inside of him felt as if it was my own.

Char was the first one to snap out of her shock and she rushed to round the counter to stand next to me. Her arm was already elbow-deep in her bottomless tote, probably searching for a potion to throw at the stalkers while I frantically looked around and counted the poor souls that would get caught in the crossfire. We never fooled ourselves into thinking we wouldn't be found in the store. We just dumbly believed Dimitri's father, or whoever else was in cahoots with him, would practice little caution and try not to kill us at noon in a store full of humans.

I wanted to smack myself. You'd think a killer would follow some decorum and ask us politely where we would like to take our last breath. Obviously, the mages' attack in the middle of the day at the pier full of tourists and locals didn't teach us anything about the type of monsters we were dealing with.

Both brutes sauntered inside the store like they owned the place, breaking me out of my internal musings. The second the sun no longer hid their features I knew what they were. A sudden spike in my heartbeat told me I was awed to be in their presence while my subconscious was screaming danger at me. At the same time my mind was screaming at me "*What are they? What are they?*"

I would've known by the way they stepped in too. Shifters had that way of walking like they were doing the earth a favor by placing their human feet on it. Predatory and animalistic. Humans do not have that much control over every single muscle in their body.

"Dimitri, if these are your buddies, now would be the right time to share that info. I'm about to lose my shit and we both know nothing good comes from that," I muttered under my breath for his ears only. "And keep an eye on Char, my insurance won't cover it if my business gets blown up by magic potions."

My friend already had a small glass jar in her left hand that was filled to the brim with some dark, purplish fluid and dangling by her side ready to be launched. She was eying the shifters with a manic grin too. At times like these, I was grateful she was on my side.

"Well?" I prompted the alpha who was frozen in place like I haven't spoken, his eyes locked on the two newcomers. "Do you know them?"

"No." The growl in his already deep voice made a cold sweat wash over me. In reaction to that my spine was so straight, I felt like I could snap in half by the softest breeze from the tension. "The two of you stay here. I will deal with them."

"Like hell you are," I said between clenched teeth, but he simply ignored me. "What kind of shifters are they?" Both were too thin to be wolves or bears, so I was assuming that they were some sort of a feline. It felt like my guess was wrong but nothing better came to mind.

The one on the left grinned back at Char, his mouth stretching wider than it was natural.

"Hyenas." Char and I both gasped at the same time.

"*Cruthaich cearcall dìon*," Create a circle of protection, I blurted without missing a beat.

Sparkles burst between the shifters and the three of us, and the air thickened and charged as the scent of ozone filled my nostrils. My fingers tingled by my sides while my magic worked, snapping tight around the three of us and sealing the protective circle as I commanded it.

Hyenas were among the bottom feeders of the supernatural world and they were easy to hire for cheap. Not because they didn't know what they were doing, mind you. They were the most skilled assassins to have on your payroll, but they didn't charge much because they took more pleasure than they should from killing anyone. All my hopes of finding out if anyone else was in on Dimitri's father's plan went down the drain. Hyenas were vicious but dumber than a box of rocks. The confused expressions on their faces as they cocked their heads to stare at the protective dome formed around us was a dead giveaway to the nonexistent IQ they had.

All muscle and no brain.

"We have to get these people out of here." Without turning her way I elbowed Char to get her attention.

The shifters were getting the attention of everyone in the store and most were inching away from them on pure survival instinct. A couple, much to my dismay, crept closer all googly-eyed. If we don't do something soon, we'll end up with MPO agents crawling all over the place.

"I can remove one or two for you if you don't mind, Little Red." The one on the left finally spoke, gracing us with another smile full of teeth.

"That reference is getting old," I grumbled under my breath shooting daggers through my slitted eyes at him.

"Get out." Dimitri bit the words out slightly louder than a whisper and the shift in energy was so sudden that I had to fight the urge to turn around and bolt out of there. An eerie glow burned behind Dimitri's irises, turning his grey eyes into living, breathing storms, tendons strained in his neck, stretching his skin, and his fisted hands shook slightly from the effort he exerted not to shift.

"We have no quarrel with you, wolf," The second hyena spoke, his voice so raw and raspy that you'd think he chewed on glass every day for breakfast. "We will take the little ladies off your hands and no one needs to get hurt."

"If I wasn't so pissed right now I would gloat for being called little for a month." Char snorted, yet her feet shuffled uneasily.

"*Ya slomayu vas oboikh, durak.*" Ignoring both of us, Dimitri took a step toward the hyenas.

A pleasant shiver worked its way up my spine when I heard him speak his mother's language. He could've asked them about the weather as far as I was concerned, but to me, it sounded like he told them that he will rip them to shreds. It was harsh, chopped, and sounded angry. It didn't help that his body language relayed that message too, so I couldn't be sure. All I knew was that I was feeling warm and tingly in places I shouldn't be feeling it. My magic was responding to the shifter's alpha power in its primal state like a moth would react to a flame.

There was something seriously wrong with me.

"Do not make me repeat myself. Get. Out." The alpha took one more step, then another before I realized he was about to exit the protection I placed around the three of us.

I should've been more worried about the humans still loitering around the store but selfishly I didn't. If given a chance, they would be the first to grab pitchforks and burn me alive if they knew what I was. I wanted them safe, sure, but if it came between those I care about and them…Guess where my loyalties would be?

I was a witch, not one of their saints.

Without thinking, I reached over the counter and

grabbed Dimitri's arm, trying to yank him back. Emphasis on tried. A truck pulling on him wouldn't have moved him an inch with the way he was poised to rip into the two dummies thinking they had safety in numbers.

However, much to my surprise, the moment my fingers made contact with his skin his whole demeanor changed. Tense muscles relaxed under my grip and he stepped sideways, placing himself directly between me and the two shifters yet he turned his head so I can see half of his face. They were no longer his priority, it was written all over his features. Neither the hyenas nor Char missed the subtle way he showed that I mattered to him. The look the two hyenas gave each other after his reaction confirmed it.

We were screwed.

Something inside me cracked, almost like a physical sensation of things rearranging themselves in my chest. Panic gripped me that I'd have to acknowledge it, so I had to do something to avoid thinking about it. Learning what we could from the shifters was far more important than what I felt when it came to the alpha.

It was.

Honest.

"I'm sorry for the inconvenience, but we must close the store for the day!" I spoke as loud as I could, grumblings following my words. "They found a gas leak at a couple of stores down from here, so for your safety, we need to let the inspectors do their job."

People were already rushing out the door, a couple of them still carrying whatever they were holding in their hands with them. I didn't care. I just wanted all the humans away so that we can deal with the two shifters who dared to come to our store.

What was funny was the fact that my declaration took

the hyenas by surprise long enough for almost all the humans to spill out of the store. Almost but not quite all, unfortunately.

"I think I'll keep this one," the one on the left, with the nightmarish grin said just as a middle-aged lady was rushing past him. Her shriek sent my heart into a gallop. "It makes us even, no? Three of you against the three of us."

He yanked her between him and his buddy, jostling her messy bun, which leaned crookedly toward her left ear and the crystal ball I didn't notice she had in her hand until it plunged toward the floor, shattering into a million pieces the moment it hit it. Wide, pale blue eyes met mine and I remembered her. She came to the store often for lavender incense and candles to help her sleep at night. She shared one day that her nightmares didn't let her stay asleep longer than an hour or two. I had no idea why I found that important to remember, but it was.

Rage bubbled up, burning hot and heavy in my chest.

"Let the woman go."

Both Dimitri and Char looked at me strangely when I spoke. It took a beat for my brain to register that what I heard was actually me speaking and not some entity that dropped in unannounced. My voice was much deeper, as if coming from a well, and carried a spine-chilling echo that brushed over my memories feather light and I forgot about it the second it was gone.

Finally, the gravity of the situation dawned on the two hyenas when the façade of their strengths became their weakness. All mockery washed off their faces with the realization that the hunters just became the prey because they bit off more than they could chew when they stepped in and threatened us.

"Ummm, Allie." Char inched cautiously closer to me,

her fingers hovering just out of reach above my shoulder. "We need to make sure the lady leaves first."

My vision was sharpening on the two shifters while I struggled to keep the rage under control so it didn't explode out of me in a wave of magic, which would destroy everything and hurt Char and the alpha in the process.

"Release the human, peasant swine. Don't make me repeat myself." Dimitri's snarl forced the two to take a couple of steps back and dragging the woman along with them, the blonde on the right turning his head left and right in search of escape routes no doubt. "I will handle this one, *malen'kaya ved'ma*."

If I wasn't freaking out that I might kill innocent people I would've laughed at the swine insult. I had no control over my body or how he made me feel, but you could bet any amount of magic that I had control of my actions and what I can and cannot do. Hot or not, the alpha was off-limits, so he had no right to boss me around and tell me to let him handle things. It's not like we were a couple or had any chance of becoming one any time soon.

For now, an annoying voice chirped in my head.

"Please!" The woman cried out for the first time, drawing me back to the moment, each of her tears like a hot poker in my brain. "Don't hurt me...please." Her sobs were gut-wrenching as she srunk into herself, her shoulders curling inward to better protect her now that only one of them had a hold on her.

There was more to the terror in her tone than the fear of the shifter who had her dangling from his grip like a bone. Whatever it was, that was the reason I held back from zapping the dumbasses because I didn't want to scare her mora than she already was, as much as I wanted to tell

Dimitri otherwise. The poor woman was traumatized long before the hyenas stepped into my store.

The hyena on the right shifted to his animal, his elongated head reaching the woman's chest.

"Oh, dear Lord, please, I don't want to die." The lady bawled even harder, closing her eyes and shaking like a leaf. "This is not happening. Please, God, this is not happening."

"I'm tired of this crap. I'll grab the woman, you two deal with the bastards." Char cocked her arm back, the one she held the glass jar full of purplish liquid with, and let the it fly through the air. It hit the floor between the shifters almost at the same spot where the crystal ball shattered. I tensed up like a spring waiting for whatever was about to happen.

Nothing happened for a moment.

Then the hyena on all fours shrieked so loud, I thought my ears started bleeding. His butt smacked into the shelf next to him and sent it tumbling into the rest of the displays. A cacophony of sounds followed for a long moment that stretched between us until it cut off abruptly and the only thing left was the panting of the shifted hyena.

A second later a nest of black snakes showed up, hypnotically curling around each other right in front of the human. Dozens of heads were snapping at the shifters simultaneously, surprisingly staying away from the woman but aiming their attacks at the shifters. Both males blenched like they've seen a ghost, their eyes bugging out with expressions of pure terror as they looked ready to get out of their own skins.

Apparently, all we needed was serpents to deal with hyenas.

Who knew?

Chapter Four

Char didn't wait to see if we agreed with her offhanded comment from earlier. As soon as her potion manifested into the creepy snakes she snapped into motion. Taking hold of her signature, black, floor-length dress in both hands she yanked it up and bolted for the human, her chestnut curls bouncing over her shoulders. The woman was all soft curves, boobs, and swaying hips, but she could make an Olympic sprinter jealous. The sorceress was as fast as a bullet. Focused on her, I almost missed the blonde hyena hunching down and preparing to pounce on my friend.

My heart jumped and hit the roof of my mouth and my fists clenched by my side.

"*Èirigh san adhar!*" Rise in the air! I barked out the spell, not caring if anyone sees me through the wall of glass that was the store front, my hand reaching for the hyena on all fours with my palm up. Magic burst from my fingertips and lifted the jerk away from my friend flinging him to the side into one of the shelves.

"Don't you dare!" Dimitri snarled from next to me and threw himself at the shifter on our left, tackling him into the remaining shelves in the center of my store just as Char made a grab for the woman.

The shifter still on two feet turned his attention to the bigger threat that was Dimitri, losing his hold on the human, thankfully. The woman jumped into Char's arms, sinking her nails into my friend's shoulders hard enough to break the skin. Char's loud hiss made me livid although I couldn't blame the human at all. The woman was sobbing so hard, my heart hurt.

Crystals, porcelain, and glass spread out all over the vinyl floors, sending shards everywhere when the two males collided. I bet blonde had no idea the wolf was going to play fetch with him that day when he woke up. Grunts and flesh hitting flesh followed the tinkling of the shattered statues when fists started flying faster than human eyes could track them, but I didn't have time to worry about the loss of merchandise. My focus was on the two shifters in front of me, now that the woman and Char were relatively out of danger. My friend dragged the woman away from the two fighting males and out of reach from the dark haired hyena. I felt like sagging from relief but we werenot out of the woods just yet.

Dimitri, who shifted mid-jump, had the blonde guy pinned to the ground, snarling and growling as he bared his sharp teeth in his face. I could see the fear in the hyena's eyes while he struggled to break free from the alpha's grip. Dimitri was formidable when dressed in a nicely pressed suit. Pissed-off Dimitri was someone everyone should avoid at all costs. Yes, he's on our side, but even I'm smart enough to be intimidated and not to get too close to the large black wolf.

Meanwhile, the guy on the right had shifted back to his human form, his eyes darting frantically around the store as he searched for either a weapon or an escape route, but there was no way out for them now. Not before they fessed up to everything we needed to know.

Char cradled the woman in her arms away from the two shifters while standing in the middle of the snakes that were still slithering on the floor in a giant, black ball of writhing bodies.

"Let him go," I said to the wolf, my voice cold and steady as I walked over to the shifters wrestling each other. "I want to make sure they regret coming here today, right after they tell us who sent them."

The male's eyes widened in fear as he saw me vibrating from the rage clawing my insides. I could feel the magic building, crackling around me, and thickening up with each passing second as it lifted strands of my hair to dance around my face on an invisible breeze.

Dimitri shifted back to his human form with a grunt of pain, still holding the hyena down with ease. He looked at me with concern, knowing the kind of destruction I was capable of when pushed to my limits, no doubt remembering the battle we had with the mages not that long ago.

Unfortunately, I couldn't hold back anymore.

These two came into my store, threatened those I care about, and caused chaos in front of the humans. They needed to learn their lesson.

Lifting my hands, I felt the energy building inside of me, thrashing and churning like a living thing. The air crackled with magic as I chanted words for a spell I'd never seen or heard before under my breath. A violet shell of swirling energy started collecting and pooling at my fingertips while a strange scent permeated the air around us, burning my nose with the stench of chared wood and smoldering ashes. The taste of iron flooded my mouth and a low hum sounded in my ears, similar to that of an engine warming up.

The tightness in my chest spread to my arms, my hands tingling as the power increased.

I found it difficult to breathe yet forced myself to remain calm or there was no telling what could happen.

The shifter underneath Dimitri started to whimper and plead for mercy while he struggled to break free, his nails ripping off as he clawed at the floor after he managed to turn to his belly.

But it was too late. Not just for them, but for my friends too.

Whatever this thing was inside of me, it was already in motion with a mind of its own.

It released very suddenly, unleashing a wave of energy that sent all of us flying backward in all directions, crashing into whatever displays of candles and incense were left. The impact shook the entire store, sending the register and the glass counter tipping over and tumbling down with a deafening crash.

"Holy crap," I breathed out, scrambling up on all fours to peer around a broken column of a shelving unit. "Did I just do that? What in all the worlds is going on?" My voice trembled and a hint of hysteria was noticeable in the high-pitched tone.

A shiver raced up and down my overheated body because whatever magic came out of me was a bone-chilling, arctic blast, blanketing everything with snow and coating the vast space white. It only left me burning up as if I had a fever.

"Allie!" Char called out from somewhere to my right,

her tone filled with worry. It was impossible to see with all the white and the dust from broken shelving still floating in the air. "We need to move this somewhere else. There are humans gathering on the street taking photos with their phones."

Just then, the door flew open and a crowd of people started flooding in, some with their phones still up in the air to capture what was happening. The blast of power coming from me and all the noise as I destroyed our store while it shook and trembled must've gotten the attention of passersby.

"Is everyone okay?" a gentleman called out, rushing in with concern while scrunching up his features. "Anyone hurt? Miss? Are you hurt, Miss?"

"Get your hands off me, human," Char snapped, and I almost laughed at her annoyance while the man gawked at her for referring to him as human as if she was an alien.

The stunned expressions from those following behind the worried samaritan told me they had no idea what they were walking into, although it seemed curiosity still got the better of them. Leave it to people from LA to care more about drama than their safety. They even dodged between shelves and stepped over piles of broken glass as they approached us cautiously.

The telltale wails of police sirens reached us from the distance, but that did not seem to stop anyone from piling into the store. I could feel hundreds of eyes on me like ants crawling all over my skin. My breathing was becoming faster and panic was starting to settle in. I managed to crawl over to the blond shifter who was laying on the floor, so I could whisper frantically to him and none of the humans could hear our conversation. Unfortunatelly the snow and dust settled already so we were there to see by everyone.

Dimitri stood up slowly, his wolfish features still visible, even in his human form. He looked at me with an intensity that almost felt like he reached a hand and settled whatever fear was building in the center of my chest. It grounded me like nothing else would've. If I wasn't mistaken, I believed the alpha used the compulsion he would normally apply to one of his pack to snap me out of a full-blown panic attack. It was frightening how much power had poured out of me and I knew he was aware of that fact, too. His eyes darted toward the shifter who hadn't moved for several moments now, undoubtedly wondering if he'd killed him by accident.

Looking at the same shifter, I doubt the hyena would move an inch out of fear I'll send another blast. Judging by the terror twisting his features, he knew I'd be sending it directly at him the second time.

Grateful for his help, I shook my head slightly, as if to reassure him we could deal with whatever the situation is before turning my attention back to the two hyenas on the floor. Keeping my tone low I made sure none of the humans could hear me.

"You two are going to answer some questions for us now, and if you say one word to any human I promise you dying will be the least of your worries," I said through gritted teeth as rage began to boil inside me all over again. Dimitri saddled closer to me and placed his hand on my shoulder, lending his support and stopping me from trying to turn into a supernova again. "You're going to tell us everything we need to know."

The hyena looked up at me with fear and desperation pooling in his eyes. All his bravado left the building after my dumb display, which could cost me my life if anyone saw me casting the spell.

"We were hired to take you out," he stuttered out while

his voice trembled. "We don't know who hired us, only that we were offered a large sum of money to do it."

I frowned, not entirely satisfied with his answer. "Who offered you the money? Who contacted you," I pressed, my voice low and dangerous, some remnants from the echo still present in it. Ants were crawling under my skin making me want to throw my head back and scream until I'm raw.

The second hyena whimpered when he tried to crawl away, finally moving and writhing in pain from where a piece of wood had managed to pierce his side. My eyes narrowed on him and his whimper sounded even more ridicilous.

Pathetic.

"I don't know," he gritted out through clenched teeth, gripping his injury while tears streamed down his face. "I swear, we were just told to find you and kill you. The two of you, not him." He tipped his chin to indicate that Dimitri apparently was too good to be killed by hyenas.

I sighed, feeling frustrated and overwhelmed. Apart from the alpha's father, I didn't know who could possibly want me dead, or why, unless this person knew I was a witch. Something I was hoping was still a secret kept between me, Char, Damian, and the alpha. I knew, however, that whoever it was, the person was knowledgeable enough to send two skilled, albeit dumb assassins, after us. Lucky for us, between me, Char, and Dimitri we packed enough power to battle an army if need be, but that did not make the hyenas any less skillful as killers.

"We need to leave," Char spoke urgently and rounded the pile of debris, grabbing my arm and pulling me towards the back exit of the store. "The police are almost here and we can't risk being here when they arrive with Allie lit up like a sprinkler for fourth of July. We'll find somewhere safe to regroup and figure out our next step." She glanced around, as if seeing the store for the first time. "I destructed the humans by making sure they know how the asilents traumatized the woman. They'll take care of her. Let's scram." I had no idea how she managed to keep her purse intact, yet there it was, the tote swinging on her shoulder with not even a speck of dust on it.

Dimitri nodded, his face set in a grim determination and a muscle ticking in his jaw. Swiftly, he bent down and scooped the barely conscious dark haired hyena off the ground before effortlessly slinging him over his shoulder. Char and I rushed over to help with the second, locking onto an arm each and dragging him into the alley behind the store. The snow from the spell had already started to melt, but it was still solid enough to hear our feet crunching through it as we moved. The group of humans were gathered around the still crying woman, oblivious to us sneaking out.

Dear stars, please make the snow melt fast. There would be no way of explaining permanent snow that lasts for months to the human police or MPO if they found it spread out in the middle of summer like it's the normal season for it. A potion made by a sourceress or snow made by a mage would dissipate within ten to twenty minutes. Anything longer will be screaming witch louder than the approaching police cars.

As soon as we were outside, the cold hit me like a ton of bricks, forcing my teeth to chatter. It was like walking into a freezer, the temperature dropping rapidly as the snow continued to fall in large, fist-sized snowflakes in the middle of LA. I shivered, wishing I could wrap my arms around myself, though more from fear of being discovered by the MPO than the cold.

"Are you okay?" Dimitri asked, his voice laced with concern as soon as my hands were free from the deadweight of the shifter.

My head bobbed to say I was, but the truth was I was so far from okay, I didn't think I would ever feel it. "I don't know how to stop this." My hand waved at the snowflakes listlessly.

"Who said that you should?" I peeked over at him and his stormy eyes kept me a prisoner.

"It's snow," I told him slowly, like he was stupid or something. "In LA."

"The elemental who made the snow managed to escape," Dimitri told me simply.

"What elemental?" Confused and drained, I blinked at him.

"Exactly." He let loose a chuckle before dropping the shifter at his feet. "You two stay here, I'll bring my car around."

And he was off.

"What elemental?" I mouthed to Char who was doing a poor job of pretending not to laugh at me.

Chapter Five

Dimitri stuffed the two shifters in the trunk of the car with zero explanation when he brought his vehicle around to the back alley of our store, and they didn't make a peep about it. I could hear them mumbling something at that moment but it was too low for my ears to make any sense of it. Maybe hyena shifters weren't as dumb as the rumors said they were but neither Char nor I said a word either.

We weren't as dumb as we looked, as well.

I absently listened to Char and the alpha talk from the spacious back seat of the Lexus, my lower body sinking and melting into the butter-soft leather. The two of them became bosom buddies in the last couple of weeks, which rubbed me wrong in so many ways for no particular reason. The fact Char lost a very important memory so she can save my hide when I screwed up, made sure I kept my mouth shut about it. It ate at me what they discussed when I wasn't within ear shot, or more precisely if they talked about me. Being an adult means I acted like one on occasion.

I also refused to ask Char.

The city was a blur that passed by as I watched unseeing through the window, my mind racing with other things instead of the guilt that's been trying to suffocate me lately. If anyone thought being on a kill list had no pros, I could've assured them that they were absolutely wrong. I for one was grateful for it, as things stood. It gave me other things to think about instead of how I messed up the lives of those around me simply by breathing.

In reality, I didn't need any additional complications; yet my intuition was a hot poker in my sternum ensuring I paid attention.

Something was really off about the whole thing.

Bell senior was much more refined and sophisticated in his approach of plotting a murder or setting up someone's destruction. Hiring hyenas to come and attack us in broad daylight was seriously not his style from what I gathered about him. The old male probaby felt smug as shit and secterly rejoyced at how elegantly and smoothly he slid the dagger between our ribs.

As we drove deeper into the city, I couldn't help but feel a sense of unease settling in my stomach. The reality was sinking in and I knew that whoever wanted us dead wouldn't give up so easily. Obviously, the lowlife had no problem delivering low blows or harming humans in the process. Aggited, I yanked my cell from my pocket when it chirped.

We needed to find answers and fast before it was too late.

"Damian will be waiting for us at the hotel," I said, and tucked my phone in the back pocket after pressing send on the text. "He said he might have something to help us get the information about who could be behind this."

Char twisted in the passenger seat to look at me and

nodded, no doubt as grateful for any lead we could get as I was. "I don't understand why the two of you trust this guy so much but as I promised, I'm not going to ask too many questions for now. Do you think the person who hired the hyenas knows about you being a witch?" she asked, her voice barely above a whisper.

"It's possible. We cannot rule it out," the alpha spoke up clutching the steering wheel as if he wanted to strangle it, his eyes on the road ahead. "But we can't jump to conclusions just yet. We need to find out everything we can from the hyenas before we make any assumptions."

The wolf seemed restless as he shifted in his seat, his animal making itself known occasionally through the glow in his irises every time he glanced at the rearview mirror and our gazes met. Char, on the other hand, seemed eerily calm - almost too calm. I couldn't tell if it was a facade or if she started forming some sort of plan already. The sorceress seemed locked in some internal dialogue, so I left her to it.

The rest of the way we stayed silent, all of us lost in our own thoughts. Our arrival at the hotel and our trek up to the room were also uneventful, thank the stars. The only hiccup occurred in the few minutes Dimitri and I had to stand guard so Char could drop a sleeping potion on the shifters. They'd stay in la la land until she wakes them up with another. I didn't feel bad at all that we left them in the trunk like some badgage.

It wasn't a surprise that Damian was already waiting for us, his dirty blonde hair tussled, seated in a comfortable armchair with a book in his hand. The writing on his skin twisted and turned where the sleeve was lifted higher up on his forearm but he covered it up as if he knew I was watching.

"Hey, nice to see you again." Char chirped as soon as we entered the room like she was talking to a stranger.

Damian looked up from his book and set it down on the small table next to him, his features set in stone. If it hurt him that the sorceress didn't recognize him, although he didn't show it. All my senses came alive the moment their eyes met. The ticking of the clock on the wall, the rustle of pages as he pressed the book on the side table, the distant sounds of traffic on the streets. All those sounds were drowned out from the blood rushing into my ears the next second.

Dimitri pressed a hand to my lower back which pulled me out of whatever it was that was happening to me.

"I've been doing some poking around and it seems like we have bigger problems than questioning your hyenas." Damian didn't waste breath on pleasantries. "There's a group of witches who have been causing trouble in the supernatural community the last forty-eight hours," the Druid said, his tone serious.

"Witches?" I gasped, my heart nearly punching out of my chest. "What kind of trouble?" My voice cracked as I asked, feeling a knot form in my stomach, tightening with each breath.

That was bad. Really, really, bad.

"They've been targeting powerful supernaturals and trying to eliminate them," Damian explained, his gaze steady on Dimitri as if daring him to contradict him. "There are rumors on the black web that they're trying to gain more power for themselves and integrate into society. But I'm sure the wolf shared that info with you ladies."

"It can't be connected." I blurted out, feeling sick. "Why would they want me dead? I didn't know there were any witches left apart from me until just now."

Damian's eyes narrowed as he regarded me, his lips pursed in contemplation. "It's hard to say for sure, but it's not uncommon for witches to target others within their own kind to eliminate competition. Your kind was not known for being friendly even among themselves."

I couldn't believe what I was hearing. There was a chance my own kind was trying to kill me? The realization hit me like a ton of bricks, and I had to sit down on the bed before my legs gave out from underneath me.

"What are we going to do?" I asked Char, my voice barely louder than a breath.

"Kill them if they are after you." My bestie's tone suggested that I'm daft for even asking that question.

Tears prickled my eyes.

Dimitri stared passively at Damian, his clenched jaw the only indication he was still fuming from the ordeal in the store. "We have to interrogate the hyenas first," he growled. "We can ponder other options for discovering more about these supposed witches later." Eyes narrowed, he had skepticism written all over his face about the information the Druid shared with us. "That is, if there really are witches behind these rumors and not just smoke screens to divert our attention away from wherever the danger is coming from."

"And what about me?" Char spoke up, her eyes flashing with internal fire that meant heads were about to roll. "They came after me, too. I want to come face to face with the brave souls who want me dead to show them how it's done."

The alpha turned to her, his eyes dancing with mirth. "We'll make sure you're safe," he mockingly promised. "No witches will be harming you on my watch, Miss Marietti."

Char laughed good-naturedly, punching him in the shoulder.

I couldn't help but feel the stab of jealousy as it washed over me at the way Dimitri was looking at Char. Open and unguarded. I know it was irrational, plus I had no right to feel that way anyway, but I couldn't help myself. Char was my best friend, my only friend in this whole mess, and the thought of her falling in love with the alpha made my blood run cold. Damian's face mirrored how I felt.

Unfortunately, we had more pressing matters to attend, too. We needed answers and we needed them fast if we wanted to survive whatever was coming our way. Urgency was building in my chest and I knew as well as I knew my own name that shit was about to hit the fan and I'd be in the middle of it…again.

Another thought pushed its way through all the others clouding my mind.

"Is that what you wanted to talk to me about in private this morning?" I asked Dimitri and I knew I was right when his shoulders stiffened making him look taller than he already was. "You heard about these witches resurfacing, didn't you?" The accusation was loud and clear in my tone.

The alpha said nothing, but he kept his steady storm blue gaze on me unblinking.

"You should be happy he didn't start discussing witches in the middle of the store." Typical Char, she always found a way to justify behavior for those she cared about. My bestie had no clue that the wolf did discuss witches in that very store a minute or two before she came to work. "Good for you to want to get her out for lunch. If I didn't know her better I would've thought she was a mole in her past life. She's scared of people and likes to hide in a hole."

"I am not!" The rebuttal was automatic and it annoyed

me enough that I bit the inside of my cheek. Char had a way of reducing me to a toddler at times.

"On the bright side," oblivious to my anger, she waved a hand in my face. "at least you didn't get a surprise visit by one of your long-lost sisters without being aware of their existence."

Something nudged the back of my mind and I frowned at my feet. A second later it socked me hard enough I almost fell off the bed I was sitting on as my head snapped up and I looked at Dimitri wide-eyed.

"Damn it!" A string of profanities poured from my lips, juicy enough to make a sailor proud. Char appeared proud too judging by the impressed expression she wore. "She was a witch, wasn't she?" The question was for the alpha who seemed to come to the same conclusion as me.

"The candle..." Dimitri trailed off.

"I knew there was something off with her but she tricked me anyway." A new wave of anger churned in my gut. "I got too worked up thinking she held the poor guy with her by using potions or spells, it didn't cross my mind that she was testing me."

The triumphant look on swan lake's face danced in my mind's eye mocking me.

"What time did you notice the hyenas following you?" The alpha asked my best friend.

"It's fifteen minutes to the store and I was half way there when I felt them creeping up from a distance." Forehead puckered in confusion, Char's gaze darted from me to Dimitri and back. "It took me another ten to fifteen when I tried to circle and double back in hopes I would lose them. Why?"

"She would've had enough time to make a call and

move the hyenas into a position to stake out your house after she left." Dimitri swore under his breath.

"I'd hate to be that person but care to enlighten the rest of us?" Damian drawled but I couldn't even be annoyed at his tone.

I was too busy freaking out.

Dimitri, with a heavy sigh told them what happened that morning when he came to the store. About the woman, about the candle, even about me hitting my elbow because I was trying to run away from him while telling him to go away. Any other day I would've laughed about how put out by that fact he was. It became obvious Dimitri Bell was not accustomed to women trying to get away from him.

"We can find her." My exclamation got their attention. "She paid with a credit card"

"Unless it was a fake one." Char mumbled while gnawing on her lower lip. "Still, it's a good lead." She looked around and frowned. "I'll need a computer to check the account number she used to pay."

"I'll be right back." Damian perked up at the mention of technology. "I might not be able to help much with other things, but computers I can do."

Chapter Six

The daylight was gradually darkening, the bright rays that used to peek through the parted curtains of the hotel room turning into a reddish orange glow of a sunset. Shadows stretched over the polished floors, since thanks to Dimitri, we were hiding in luxury; unlike our dingy motel the first time Char and I got attacked. No smelly, stained covers on single beds for the alpha.

Speaking of which, the sorceress extraordinaire was hunched over the thin laptop Damian brought in from his car a couple of hours ago. Searching for the information on the woman who purchased the candle that morning proved to be more difficult than expected. The Druid and my friend had their heads close together as they conversed about things which sounded alien to me.

I, on the other hand, did my best to ignore Dimitri and his proximity to me by inspecting the thread on the oriental rug. Very mature, I know.

Suddenly, a triumphant sound escaped Char's lips, startling all of us. She spun towards me, her hand over her mouth and her eyes glowing with excitement. "I found her! The woman who bought the candle!" She exclaimed, practically bouncing up and down in her seat.

Damian was frowning at the laptop, his eyes darting over the text I couldn't see from where I was sitting cross-legged on the bed. Dimitri didn't believe in personal space so he leaned in over me to take a look at the screen, his arms resting on my shoulders as he used his damn shifter vision to read from that far. I tried not to shrink away at the contact, but it was hard. I could feel the heat of his body on my back, his scent filling my nostrils.

It was fogging my mind.

"The name of the woman who bought the candle is Isadora De La Cruz," Char said as she typed away on the keyboard with the Druid keeping a close eye on her every move. "And get this - she's been arrested before for practicing witchcraft by the human police when she set a house on fire! In Louisiana."

My heart skipped a beat at her words, and I felt myself grow pale. "That's too far of a drive just to buy a candle," I said, my brows furrowing in confusion while I did my best to ignore the fact Dimitri was rubbing soothing circles on my back. It worked to calm me too damn him. "What does all this mean for us?" I asked the room, addressing no one in particular. "They are fakes?"

"It means we need to be careful until we know exactly what we are up against and what is going on," Dimitri said, his voice low and soothing.

Char nodded in agreement. "We'll keep digging and see what else we can find out about her."

I nodded slowly, taking deep breaths to calm myself down. The thought of being exposed to the MPO for who I was, was terrifying to say the least. But having witches resurface out of nowhere? It added yet another layer of danger in my already overwhelming life.

"We should contact the coven," Char said suddenly, breaking the silence. "They must have a coven, right?" She blinked at me as if expecting me to be an expert on it. Just because I was born a witch didn't mean I knew anything about it. I mean, I didn't know squat about it honestly.

"Coven? Are you crazy?" I asked, my eyebrows shooting up to my hairline at the insanity. How would I know if they have a coven? Last time I checked I was the only witch still breathing."

"Well, we need their help," my bestie replied firmly. "Witches, hello! They would know more about your magic than the two of us put together, and they might be able to help us figure out how to fix..." trailing off she looked pointedly at the alpha "...our other problem."

Fingers crossed Dimitri might think she's talking about his father and not his engagement. I didn't want to poke at a sleeping lion until I was sure I could break the oath that was forced on him.

After a long hesitation, I nodded reluctantly. "Okay," I said. "But how do we contact them? And what makes you think they'll talk? Did you forgot they sent the hyenas to kill us? "

Char grinned. "No, I didn't forget." Yanking Damian closer, she cuddled his arm between her boobs stroking it lovingly and batting her lashes. "But they don't know we have a Druid. If they don't play nice he can block their powers."

"He can?" I mumbled, eying the poor Druid and tensing up to jump and catch him if he fainted.

Char was clueless of Damian's reaction; the blanching of his face and the widening, wild look in his green eyes. I felt horrible having to come to his rescue, while Dimitri snickered in the poor male's face. I was grateful he stapped away from me a minute before that, so I didn't comment on it.

"Unhand the Druid, Char." My lips curled slightly in a reassuring smile when Damian's gaze snapped to me. "I don't think he is used to being treated like a house cat." Cocking my head I watched his Adam's apple bob up and down. "Scratch that, I don't think he is used to being touched at all." I amended my assessment.

Dimitri coughed to cover his laugh, so I smacked him on the arm with the back of my hand. "Ouch," he grumbled, rubbing his bicep as if he could feel it. "What was that for?"

"For laughing at Damian's expense," I scolded, crossing my arms over my chest and daring him to continue. "It's not funny."

He rolled his eyes but didn't argue with me. Instead, he turned to Char. "So, how do we find this coven?"

Her smile faltered as she pulled away from Damian's arm much to the Druid's relief. The poor male slumped in his seat like a deflated balloon. "I don't know," she admitted, running a hand through her hair. "But I have an idea."

She turned to me, a mischievous glint in her eyes. "Remember that book your mom gave you?"

Out of habit since I'd been hiding what I am my whole life, my heart skipped a beat and a wave of terror washed over me. "What book?"

"The one with spells and rituals," Char said impatiently, again oblivious of the effect her comment had on me. "The one you keep under your bed?"

I nodded, finally calming my fight or flight survival

instincts and knowing what she was getting at was a tool we needed. "You want me to use a spell from that book?"

Side-eying the alpha and the Druid, I wasn't surprised they had zero reaction to our conversation about my family grimoire, or as I'd like to call it, my mother's journal. They knew my secret and it was safe with them. We had a common goal if for no other reason.

"Exactly," she said, grinning from ear to ear. "We can use a communication spell to contact the coven or a tracking spell to find their location. With a communication spell they'll be able to hear us, and we'll hear them, too, from what I've heard."

"Because you hang out with a lot of witches?" For some reason it annoyed me that we talked about it like it's an everyday occurrence.

Char gave me a deadpan look, which promptly shut me up.

"Never mind." I mumbled, feeling the heat of my face as my cheeks reddened.

Dimitri and Damian exchanged an unreadable look, and I couldn't help but feel a flicker of excitement in my chest. Contacting the coven was risky, but it was also our best chance at figuring out who was behind the assassination attempts and how the killer was connected to the old alpha. If the killer was connected to the old alpha that was.

"Okay," I said, nodding with determination. "Let's do it."

Char practically squealed in excitement and rushed to hug me tightly, whispering words of encouragement and telling me we got this. I felt a strange mix of anxiety and thrill at the thought of using a communication spell. Hell, any spell for that matter. It was the kind of magic that could go horribly wrong, but it was a risk I was willing to take.

"Let's go get the grimoire." I jumped off the bed as Dimitri and Damian started collecting our things.

We left the hotel the same way we entered, silent; Char and I were fearful, and overbearingly cautious to a point we drove the males insane. We piled up in the alpha's vehicle and returned to our apartment after Dimitri drove a few circles around the same blocks to avoid being followed. Not because they didn't know where I lived, but to delay the knowledge that we were home until we figured out the spells we needed. Dimitri's Lexus pulled up to our building, and we all silently scrambled out, each of us subtly glancing over our shoulders no doubt from the feeling of being watched we felt poking between our shoulder blades and heating up the back of our necks.

Damian assured us that he can cast a protection spell around the whole building; and although it won't stop a supernatural from attacking us if one wanted, it would slow whomever tried down. Feeling as if I had no other options available, like destroying all my enemies and freeing me from this horrible feeling, I would take what I could get. Dimitri slung the two hyenas over his shoulders and carried them up the stairs while we watched the Druid chant something low enough it was as if he was mouthing the words. Bushes and trees swayed like a snake dancing to a piper's song, and they released a collective sigh when he was finished. The only evidence that he did perform magic was the brightening of his tattoos that were writhing and flashing all over his skin, including his face. All the short hairs on my body perking up at attention that you'd think I stood next to a power reactor.

"Thank you." I told Damian. It wasn't nearly enough but there were no other words I could use to express my gratitude. He could've been seen; but to protect us he did it anyway and that meant a lot to me. Apart from Char, no one else has made an effort to have my back.

Well Dimitri did, but I refused to think about it.

"Any idea on what we are going to do with the two hyenas?" I looked between the rest of our little group. "I mean we can't just leave them hidden like a pair of dirty socks."

"The potion will keep them asleep and alive for at least a month before their body feels the strain of no food or water." Char didn't miss a beat with her answer as if she had been expecting me to ask. "Let's deal with our immediate problem and we can figure them out later."

No one disputed her comment; although it kind of bothered me a little, I let it drop. I mean they did attack me. It wasn't like I owed them anything.

I put both of them out of my mind for the time being.

As always, walking in the apartment felt like a weight was lifted off my shoulders. The fake sense of security that not long ago made me breathe a lot easier nudged at my brain but I ignored it. We had so many protections and spells around the building but they still didn't save us from the vampire attack Dimitri's father organized.

Char immediately rushed to my room and flopped onto the bed like she had done so many times before while I hurriedly retrieved the grimoire from beneath the mattress. The place was invisible to anyone else by me, the book attuned to reveal itself when it senses me near and searching for it. It was the only connection I had to my family and I hugged it to my chest for a moment as I always did just to feel its familiar energy. My fingers grazed the ancient pages until I finally released a sigh and climbed up to my feet. Finding a communication spell was not the problem, my best shot at performing one however was still up in the air.

"I think I'm going to freestyle it," I said aloud avoiding eye contact. From the corner of my eye I saw Dimitri giving me an encouraging nod as if he expected me to do exactly that the whole time.

Char on the other hand slapped her forehead and peered out from between her fingers, skepticism written all over her face. "Do you think you can just stab it in the dark?" She asked doubtfully. "I'm worried that it might backfire somehow. I'd feel better if we have some guidance." Leaning forward she grumbled something under her breath. "Maybe I should find an incantation or something and do it."

"No." All my doubts pushed aside, I rushed to prevent her from performing anymore spells or incantations that she'd had to pay for on my behalf."

Taking a deep breath, I placed the book between me and Char on the bed and held my hands above it while willing it to come to my aid. The room filled with a magical energy, and soon enough I received the answering prickle of magic coming from my grimoire.

I closed my eyes, focused on the pages and followed the thread connecting me to the ancient book. Words I couldn't understand flowed from my lips, the magic surging through my body eagerly like a puppy excited to play with its owner. The grimoire replied with a warm, loving tingle that spread from my fingertips to my toes.

Suddenly, the air around us shimmered and a soft voice echoed in my mind. "You are here."

A mysterious voice shattered the silence, like a ghostly whisper in the room. I glanced around to see if everyone else could hear it too, and found Char's face pale and motionless. Dimitri and Damian were watching me strangely but there was more curiosity than fear in their eyes.

"It's okay, the voice? It's just the book." I swallowed hard and tried to sound confident even if my heart was racing so fast I felt lightheaded. "No need to be afraid."

"Voice?" Dimitri stiffened but the woman spoke again and I tuned everything else he said out.

There was a hum thudding in my ears before the voice became clear again but I missed what it said. It sounded like it was coming from a bad reception area, which was a ridiculous thought.

The voice laughed in my mind, a soft tinkling sound as if reading my thoughts.

I winced at that possibility, but had no time to waste to dwell on idiocies. "I need your help with something." Lowering my hand I pressed my palm on the leather. "Please. It's a matter of life or death."

Chapter Seven

The grimoire responded to my plea with a surge of energy so strong that it prickled at my fingertips as if my fingers were clutching a live wire. The voice in my mind steadily grew stronger, and more eager to chat. I listened intently as it whispered sweet promises and other nonsense I couldn't understand but it was a balm for my lonely heart, feeling the weight of its words settle around me like a hug.

"Very well, kin. What do you require?" the voice asked, its tone calm and measured with a thrill of expectation in it. That should've been my first hint that nothing comes easy, or that something was off.

"I need your help in finding witches that aren't supposed to exist," I replied, my voice shaking ever so slightly from nerves as I spoke. "Last known location is Louisiana." I added it as an afterthought.

There was a pause on the other end of the connection, and I could feel the tension in the room growing as everyone held their breaths in anticipation to hear what happens while holding back all the questions I knew they had.

"Witches? And why is it that you seek them, kin? Nothing good will come of it." the voice asked, warning lacing each syllable.

I took a deep breath, trying to collect my thoughts. "There have already been attempts on my life, and I believe that they may be connected to the person who wants me dead." I explained. "I need to find them to understand their involvement. Maybe they are the ones wanting me gone. If that's the case I'd like to know why."

Once more, the room was filled with an oppressive silence until the grimoire spoke again. "Very well. I can offer you guidance, but it will come at a cost."

I felt the cold dread of resignation settle in my stomach. Nothing in the world of magic came without a price and I knew this wouldn't come for free either. Swallowing hard, I asked "What would be my price?"

"An offering," the voice replied simply, all remnants of cozying up to me gone.

"What kind of an offering?" I challenged, unwilling to give away something that meant a lot to me so easily. Although what that would be I still had not even the slightest idea.

"It has to be something of great personal value to you," the grimoire said, its tone never wavering as if it already knew I had nothing to offer and what my answer would be. If I didn't know better I would've thought it didn't want me to go looking for the woman that came to my store by asking for something I can't give.

My heart ached as I tried to recall a memory of my mother in my mind's eye and kept coming up with a black void staring at me from a vast distance – she had already been taken away from me before I was old enough to be able to remember her face, but I still desperately tried to picture something. Anything.

Char was all I had in life and there was no way in this world or another that I'd ever offer her up for anything. My gaze instinctively settled on Dimitri who was watching me intently with an unreadable expression. He had one hand gripping Damian's shoulder and the other curled around Char's upper arm. It was a very strange positioning of his body but I'd have to ask him later about it.

I paused for a moment, considering my options. There was nothing else left for me to offer - not even myself - and certainly not Dimitri who wasn't mine in any capacity besides our unlikely alliance. We both had our own motives pushing us to stick together, it wasn't like he woke up one morning and said 'you know what? I think I'll go help Alaska with her crap because she deserves it.' Yeah, Dimitri watched out for his own perky ass alright.

I took a deep breath before snorting softly to myself.

"Anything specific in mind?" I prompted the book, trying to mask the fear in my voice with a hint of sass. "Because I'll tell you now the only thing I have of value is my best friend and…well, you. And I won't offer you Char, she's off limits. Not even at the cost of my own life."

If I stopped to think about that whole situation, I would've wondered why the book I've had my entire life decided that very day to speak up when it had never done so before. Or why it felt okay to sit on the floor of my bedroom with three other people hovering over me and watching whatever exchange I had going on. But I didn't; so it continued spiraling my life down into a rabbit hole way too deep to ever escape from.

"You can offer something that is of personal value in the

future but has not yet revealed itself." The voice offered softly and thoughtfully.

"How very nice of you to try and help." I was pretty sure my face expressed my aggravation more than my tone.

Again, my gaze darted to Dimitri for a split second, long enough for my heart to skip a beat when our eyes locked. Quickly, I dropped it to my lap where he won't notice how flustered he made me feel. Or so I hoped anyway. I'd stay away from Dimitri Bell if I knew what was good for me. Nothing worth my sanity or my life will come out of it.

"Okay." I finally said on a heavy sigh. "When I have something of personal value in the future I will give it to you as an offering. I have no idea how you'll take it but I'll worry about it when the time comes."

I was getting tired. Drained was more like it judging by the way my body was hunching over, almost folding in on itself. A strange thought came to mind that it was so weird to have Char stay silent for that long but I brushed it off. She hadn't said a word since I touched the grimoire and that was beginning to worry me. Usually, my friend had a lot to say when faced with difficult situations like this one. But, it could be that we were all weirded out, tired and bruised from the ordeal that morning. Who am I to judge her if she needed some space and had no desire to talk?

Excited energy thrummed under my fingertips that were pressed on the weathered leather. If there was any ominous vibe coming from it, it must've been masked well because it almost felt like the book was sighing too as if a heavy burden was lifted off of it. The scent of old tomes and mildew saturated the air and filled my nostrils. Like the history and knowledge the book harbored, my nose detected a strong and pungent odor that smacked me in the face so unexpectedly I recoiled from it, losing the connection as my hand lifted off the cover.

My mouth opened on a silent scream when suddenly everything around me came to life. Lights flickered in the background, knickknacks seemed to be floating in mid-air and the grimoire's pages shifted as if they were being flipped through before slamming the book shut with a loud smack. So enthralled with the alluring tone of the voice, I never noticed that every other sound ceased to exist around me. It was like time had stopped, just for a moment, while everyone's attention was focused on me. As if waking up from a daunting nightmare, I gasped and dropped forward, holding myself up with my arms while fighting for breath.

"Allie." Char shouted and jerking away from Dimitri's hold, she crawled to me and gathered me in her arms. "Breathe, woman. Just breathe." My friend kept repeating.

My head ached and throbbed with stabbing pain as I stubbornly fought for consciousness. Everything around me was blurring and becoming disorienting, like a thick fog had suddenly descended into my bedroom. I heard my friend's voice but it was muffled, like she was talking from the other end of a long tunnel. The next thing I knew, her arms tightened around me as my body started shuddering uncontrollably.

Through the fog of confusion, I could hear the alpha and Damian saying something, their voices urgent but I couldn't understand a word they were saying. A train was thudding in my ears, the horn screaming so loud that I felt a trickle of warm liquid slide down the side of my face. It was then that I realized what was happening – they were trying to pull me back from some kind of trance-like state induced by the grimoire's power. How I didn't realize what was going on as it happened was beyond me.

Char kept whispering calming words in my ear, her hands rubbing my back and arms in even, soothing strokes. Meanwhile, Dimitri's lips were moving as if he was casting spells in an attempt to break any kind of magical connection that might have remained between me and the leather tome.

Suddenly, a voice broke through all the chaos surrounding us. It belonged to a mysterious, shadowy figure whose presence none of us noticed until now. He introduced himself as Zin and speaking urgently he explained that he was responsible for activating this special ability within me – an ability that would allow me access the realms beyond that what other of my kind have accomplished. Zin warned us of great risks involved in going forward and suggested that we take great care to keep it a secret.

Then he was gone and I wondered if maybe I was in a delirium and I imagined him. A hysterical giggle built in my throat because it almost sounded like the shadowy male said his name was Sin. Then nausea hit me again doubling the sound of the shrieking horn and I doubled over in Char's hold.

"Give me my purse." Char was yelling at one of them over my head where I was pressed to her chest since I was clinging to her torso like a drowning man would clutch a straw. "Hurry up!"

"Char." My lips moved but I had no clue if I whispered it or screamed it. No one paid me any attention so I tried again. "Char."

"Throw it at me damn you." She snarled at someone and both of us swayed when something hit us from the side.

"Char?" With great effort I lifted my face and blinked up at my friend when she glanced down at me.

"Breathe, Allie." Her voice broke and I frowned at the anguished expression she wore.

"I'm okay." My attempt to reassure her seemed it made it worse because fat tears rolled down her face and my heart begun to gallop. The horn was getting louder to a point of driving me insane. "Make it stop...please."

"I got you, Allie." Char choked out and pressed a potion bottle to my lips.

I didn't see her take it from her tote so in a knee-jerk reaction I tried to recoil from it but was too weak to move. Bitter fluid filled my mouth and I gagged on it hoping to spit it out. My friend grabbed my mouth so I had to swallow the potion. The last thing I remembered was giving her a look of betrayal clear enough that it made her flinch.

Good. Because the moment I woke up, we were going to have some words after I made sure the two hyenas were removed from our bathroom so I could hug the toilet for a few days.

Then my consciousness took a nosedive into a kaleidoscope of colors.

When I finally regained some sense of awareness, I found myself in an unfamiliar place that seemed like a portal between this world and another. Everything around me looked surreal and strange, like something out of a dream or nightmare; trees with trunks made of rubies, creatures with wings made of silver and gold, distant hills that moved ever so slightly like living beings beneath the night sky. It was all too much for me to comprehend and so I just stood there in shock as I tried to make sense of what was going on.

Dimitri's voice broke through the stillness and made me jump because I didn't notice anyone else with me. He explained that this place -this portal-was created by Zin using his magic and connected both, him and me, with some magical bond. From here we would be able to access secrets from my grimoire, secrets which might help us understand more about what exactly brought the alpha into my life in such an inexplicable way, and why.

With these words ringing in my ears I watched Dimitri disappear into thin air and was left to stand in the strange place all alone.

"Hello?" The moment I whispered it a hand wrapped around my neck and I passed out with my own scream echoing in my head.

Chapter Eight

"What in all the worlds did I drink last night?" Groaning I pressed the heel of my palm to my sweaty forehead over the plastered strands of hair that were practically glued to the skin there.

There was a war drum pounding behind my eyeballs; some tribal call for blood or something. My eyes were watering badly, so I had to keep them barely open. Everything was too bright.

My own voice made me flinch because it sounded like I was screaming the words from the top of my lungs, as well, even though I barely whispered them. The hangover sucked big time, so I made a mental note to never, *ever*, touch whatever alcohol I had the night before. If it was alcohol at all, since Char had these crazy ideas occasionally to mix up a fun, aka not so fun afterwards, potions that were better than anything the humans could come up with. When we had them, it felt like everything was perfect and happiness was all we knew while we walked on air, until it wore off and we crashed hard enough to be miserable close to forty-eight hours afterwords.

"Take it easy." Speaking of my friend, Char was there the second I attempted to move, brushing my soaking wet hair off my face and helping me lift myself up higher on the bed. "Here, relax into them... there you go." After fluffing the pillows, she leaned back and eyed me critically.

The fog replacing my brain lifted minutely, my mind perking up at the unusual behavior Char was displaying. She was smiling indulgently, maybe even woodenly, at me, like a doctor doing their best not to show that the patient had less than a week to live. With that thought, my heart jumped then skipped a beat before stuttering like an old Buick doing its best to get moving with a fifty-year-old rusted engine.

"I'm dying, aren't I?" I rasped through dry, numbed lips. Cold sweat trickled down my spine as I fought to remember anything that could've happened the night before. Did I get ambushed and hurt without seeing it coming? I came up blank apart from my weird dreams, which I'd rather forget.

"What?" Char recoiled in a way someone would flinch back from a leper diseased person. "Of course, you're not dying. Seriously Allie, don't be daft. I wonder sometimes how you can be considered an adult with an imagination like that."

Holy stars, I called bull-crap on everything.

I narrowed my eyes at her, lips pressed in a firm line. My heartbeat picked up pace.

"You're not dying?" My eyebrows hit my hairline when she phrased that as a question I should know the answer to. Deflating like a balloon, she buried her face in her hands. "I hope you're not dying, Allie, because if you do I'm going to find a way to bring you back so I can kill you myself, just so you know."

"That's necromancy, and you're a sorceress not a necromancer." I pointed out before frowning at her, which made my head pound worse. There was a tension at the back of my skull like some giant hand was doing its best to squeeze my head and pop it like a grape.

"You don't know what I'm capable of." She challenged indignantly.

"As a matter of fact, I do. That's what makes me your best friend, but you're deflecting. What is going on?" Stabbing a finger in the air between us I pointed it at her nose. "And don't you dare lie, Charmaine Marietti. I feel like I got hit by a truck which went back and forward a few times before I tripped and fell down a damned ravine. I'm feeling murderous."

"What do you remember?" Sighing and tucking one leg under her, she perched on the bed next to my legs fussing and rearranging her dress in a poor attempt to avoid eye contact.

"How long was I asleep?" For the first time I glanced at the window to check if it was light or dark outside. "Is that plywood? What happened to the window?" Because she ducked her head to hide deeper in the mess of curls falling over her face, I waved a hand at her although she couldn't see me. "Actually, you know what? Forget I asked, I really don't think I want to know. What day is it?"

"Wednesday." Char mumbled smoothing the fabric over her bent knee.

"Hump day. Yay! It means we survived half of the week." When my feeble stab at humor failed I nudged her with my hip. "We were nearly drowned on the beach in the middle of the day not long ago, Char. It can't be much worse. Tell me what happened and I might remember something. My head is killing me though. Let me grab an aspirin or something first."

"Stay." She barked when I tried to roll out of bed. "I'll bring whatever you need. I actually have the perfect potion for a headache."

Something about the idea of Char giving me a potion to drink tapped my brain but I felt horrible enough to ignore it. Breathing through my nose to avoid project vomiting all over the bed and myself .I burrowed deeper into the pillows so I could relax. Until a frosty breeze grazed my cheekbone feather-soft but with purpose, and a chill passed through me with such a forbidding vibe I shot up in bed like a slingshot.

"Who's there?" I rubbernecked in search of whatever it was that touched me, forgetting all about my poor head. The pain stabbed me with a vengeance for daring to ignore it out of survival instincts.

"I told you to lay back." Char mumbled disapprovingly as she returned into my room, and out of fear I'd sound like a lunatic I said nothing about ghost-fingers floating in the room with us. Chances were, I could've imagined it. "It won't kill you to listen on occasion, Allie."

After searching her face for any indication that she knew we have some invisible entities in the apartment or maybe we have a reason to worry about such things, and finding nothing, I leaned back gingerly on the pile of pillows.

"Drink this." She jabbed a long glass tube in my hand. "You'll feel like new in one second."

I stared at the liquid a moment too long it seemed because when my gaze lifted from the tube to my friend she flinched and glanced away. Slowly and deliberately I pressed the potion to my lips and tipped it back until the last drop slid past my lips. Tart blueberry flavor bloomed over my taste buds followed by a soothing honey sweet aftertaste of a cantaloupe. As she promised, the headache and any other soreness disappeared and with a sigh I sagged on the mattress from relief.

"You are a lifesaver, Char." I told her with a smile. "I never want to feel like that again. Like, ever."

"I bet you don't." Her tone was even but there was a tightness to her jaw that only showed up when Char was ready to start a headcount.

"I'm ready now for the Reader's Digest version of what happened." Patting the space next to me, I stared her down until she gave up and threw herself onto it. "Unless I was drunk enough that I called Dimitri to tell him how much I appreciate his ass, in which case, please leave me to enjoy my ignorance, I beg of you."

"I take it you don't remember the attack in the store yesterday morning?" Ignoring my childish comments, she propped her head on her hand and looked at me levelly.

I shook my head and started gnawing on the inside of my mouth.

Char proceeded to tell me in great detail about everything I couldn't recall from a little over the last twenty-four hours. I listened intently to every word all the way until she told me I'd passed out in her arms after she fed me a potion to knock me out. According to her, there was so much magic pumping through my body she was scared I'd blow all of us up.

The more she talked, the more the realization settled in my heart that my biggest fear was coming true. The curse of my kind had found me and I was going to be driven mad because I couldn't control the amounts of magic going through me. It was the exact reason witches were hunted and killed in our world. And it wasn't even the going insane part that sent my heartbeat into overdrive. It was the fact that I was a danger to Char. The only person that's been there for me through thick and thin my entire life.

"Do you remember what happened after you touched your mother's journal?" Char searched my face, her dark eyes full of concern. "You froze and zoned out so fast it was freaky to see. It was as if your soul departed your physical body. Your eyes turned fully white and all color drained from your skin." A shudder made her visibly shiver and she shook me along with the bed from it. "Dimitri had to hold me and Damian back so we didn't touch you. He said we could've hurt you with any contact and you might stay like that forever."

Tension was starting to form at my temples as I racked my brain to remember something. Surely the dreams circling like vultures in my head were just that. Dreams. But they kept being persistent, especially a memory of the alpha staring at me intently while he had one hand wrapped around Char's upper arm and another on Damian. Dimitri was many things, but touchy feely he was not. Maybe that's why that specific moment was engraved in my brain. I believed Char, but that just confirmed it, too.

"Fully aware I might sound like a crazy person, I think I talked to the book." I said and watched my friend's reaction, unblinking. "I'm sure I'll remember everything eventually but what I find more important is this witch problem you mentioned."

"They are the least of my worries." Chat waved me off.

"I think they should be our number one worry." At her frown, I hurried to explain before she brushed it off like yesterday's news. "We can defend against a known threat Char, but we can't afford an unknown one to blindside us again. If they have a record of me performing spells inside the store, we have a much bigger problem than Dimitri's father. MPO will be hunting me down."

"Dimitri will protect you from MPO, Allie. We need to find these witches and see what's going on if you think they are important." She reached across and took my stone-cold fingers in her hand. "Sometimes it breaks my heart that you think you are so unworthy of love that you don't allow yourself to notice when someone truly cares for you."

"The only thing Dimitri Bell cares about is his reputation and empire. Don't be fooled Char." The words tasted bitter in my mouth.

"If you say so." With a shrug she rolled off the bed to loom over me. "Maybe a shower will refresh your memories. Go jump in and I'll make coffee...," her voice trailed off when a knock sounded at the front door. "That's either Dimitri or that Druid. They said they'd come here as soon as they could."

Nothing could've propelled me into the bathroom faster than the mention of Dimitri. I was up and closing the door so fast you'd think my ass was on fire. Snorting at my behavior Char shook her head and headed to open the door.

"If you stay in there longer than twenty minutes I'm going to come in and drag you out naked in front of whoever is at our door." My friend threatened before laughing out loud at my pained groan. "And I'll melt the lock if I have to so don't even think of locking it. Last week I accidently made acid instead of a potion I needed so it'll be a perfect way to test it."

"You wouldn't!" I shouted incredulously through the door.

"Oh yeah?" She kept walking, I could hear her feet whispering over the wooden floors. "Try me."

"I have no idea where your soul will go, Char. Damn you." Glowering at the closed door, I started yanking on my clothing with jerky movements out of frustration. I had enough of the alpha to last me a month. Why couldn't I catch a break?

"I've been damned since the day I was born, Allie. Too late now to try and curse me." She muttered but I still heard it.

What was that supposed to mean?

Chapter Nine

Eyes closed, I stood under the harsh spray of steamy water, hot enough to melt the skin off my face. There was a chill embedded in the marrow of my bones deep enough I feared it would never go away. In a crazy attempt to feel somewhat more normal I held my breath while the spray pelted me hard enough I had no doubt my skin will be lobster red when I was done with the shower.

Also, I was prolonging seeing the alpha, as well, while being mindful of Char's warning.

I mean, I never thought that I'm the only witch alive, per se. In all honesty I kind of hoped that I'm not the only one of my kind, and Dimitri admitting his mother was one loosened a knot in my chest I didn't know was there.

"There are more." I breathed into the steam filling up the shower.

What that meant for me I had no clue; but, although they obviously wanted me dead, it still gave me some weird sense of belonging. There was a place in this world for someone like me, as twisted as my powers might be.

Loud rapid raps on the bathroom door had me jumping a foot in the air and clutching my chest in case my heart jumps out of it. With my heartbeat hammering inside my ribcage it was difficult for a moment to hear the muffled voice, so I turned the water off after a long moment since my shaky fingers kept slipping off the tap.

"What?" shouting as loud as I can I tugged the curtain and stuck my head out.

"Five minutes." Char informed me courtly. "I have coffee ready but I'll pour it down the drain while you watch if you are not out in four."

"You are a mean, mean woman, Charmain Marietti." Blinking water off my eyelashes I glared at the door.

"And don't you forget it." She snickered and her mocking laughter drifted away with her departure.

My friend was doing her best to make things seem normal for me and I was grateful for it.

It was against everything I am to eavesdrop but it'll be a lie if I said I didn't strain my ears to catch whose voice was coming from the living room along with Char's. Would it be too much to ask for it to be the Druid? As soon as the thought entered my mind guilt stabbed me so hard, it physically doubled me over.

Memories of my dreams, which I now doubted were dreams at all, made me pause. I wasn't ready to acknowledge yet that all the crazy circling inside my head happened for real but I couldn't easily dismiss it either. Before sharing it with Char, I had to think a little longer on it. However, a voice faint but clear enough to be heard whispered about paying a price with something of a great personal value and that hit too close to home with the blood magic my friend performed to save me and forgot all about Damian as a result. How much did the Druid mean to her that she sacrificed him to make sure my head stays attached to my shoulders? My time was ticking so I stepped out of the shower and wrapped a towel around my soaking wet body but my brain was going a hundred miles an hour.

My best friend and I had an agreement not to disclose information to each other that can implicate us in things which I guessed covered her rear when it came to her dealings in the magical black market. Information I found out from no other than Dimitri Bell who no doubt gloated because he knew something I didn't.

Returning to my room with a cloud of steam following my path from the bathroom to the dresser, I stabbed my legs in the jeans a bit harsher than was necessary. A few weeks ago, I blamed Dimitri for my life exploding and turning inside out, but the more time passed and new developments became clearer, the more I had to begrudgingly reconsider things.

I was becoming reckless.

With or without the old alpha gunning for his son's head someone would've eventually started paying attention to the White Kalla. The fact that witches came out of the woodwork around the same time, told me this had been long overdue.

Pointedly avoiding the boarded window, I pulled the long-sleeved t-shirt over my head and towel dried my hair so it's not plastered to my skull. The floor was cool under my bare feet yet I felt too lazy to put socks on. Something I regretted a minute later when I joined Char and the alpha in my living room. Head bowed together they were whispering something but separated fast as soon as they saw me.

"Miss McCullough." Dimitri leveled me with his penetrating, intense stare and I all but tripped over my own feet.

"Mr. Bell." I drawled back and threw the wet towel over

the back of the chair so I can snatch the huge mug full of steaming coffee my friend handed me. "I love you." I breathed and Dimitri's eyes went as wide as saucers.

"She's talking to the coffee." Char drawled and cleared her throat since it annoyed her when I draped towels around the dining table but I pretended I didn't hear her. With a huff she yanked it off the chair and stomped toward my room to probably drop it on my bed. She always did that.

"I updated Dimitri about yesterday, that you don't remember anything." My bestie tossed over her shoulder probably guessing correctly that it rubbed me wrong seeing them whispering like conspirators when I joined them.

"Nothing?" Dimitri searched my face but I only shook my head dejectedly.

"You're like a dog, aren't you?" I rushed to say before he started interrogating me, or before Char was back, as I slurped the liquid goodness just to frustrate him. "Pet it once and you can't get rid of it."

"And when was it that you petted me, malen'kaya ved'-ma?" A deep baritone rumbled in his chest as he eyed me like he wanted to melt the clothing I wore off of my body.

My mouth dried up.

"Why are you here?" I knew it was childish but it was also necessary for my sanity. I couldn't think straight even without Dimitri taunting me with his looks and smiles. Not long ago I couldn't stand the arrogant male, I had no idea what was wrong with me.

"To check on you." One eyebrow arched up as if wanting to say it was obvious, the alpha leaned forward on the loveseat.

The loveseat that resembled toy furniture when his bulk filled almost half of it.

Swallowing thickly, I instinctively took a step back.

One corner of his full lips twitched up.

"How nice of you." Smacking my hand on the ceramic to hide my nerves and almost burning myself when hot coffee sloshed over the rim of the mug, I smiled brightly at him. "You checked. Now you can go away."

"Stop being obtuse, Allie." Char sashayed back to join us, an unimpressed expression on her face. "I'm glad he is here because we can use all the help we can get."

With a sigh I rubbed a hand over my face. "I'm sorry." I told Dimitri on a huff which made both of them raise their brows as if I'd grown a second head. "I'm just very irritable today."

"Today?" Dimitri grinned when I scowled at him.

"What she's trying to say is that she's always prickly, but today we get the special Alaska treatment." Char ever the helpful woman smirked like a fiend. "Anyway, tell her what you told me, Dimitri."

After Char returned to her place next to the alpha they stared at me mutely until I shuffled over to the armchair and plopped onto it. It took me a moment to realize that instead of talking the alpha was staring at my bare feet like he's never seen toes before and I hurriedly tucked them under my butt. He looked up and blinked at me slowly.

I hid behind the mug as I kept sipping my coffee in hopes he wouldn't notice how much he unnerved me.

"After I left here, I went to check how things are with my father. To see if he may be surprised to see me yet again unharmed; to also uncover if he had something to do with yesterday's attack." A line formed between his eyebrows as his gaze became unfocused.

I glanced at Char because it was unlike Dimitri to look so off somehow. The male was always sharp and in control that it took me aback as I watched the expression solidify on his handsome face. He...He almost seemed lost.

"Did he?" My tone barely above whisper in the silence, I tilted forward on the armchair gripping the armrest with one hand for no reason. What was I thinking? That I should go hug him to make him feel better?

Ludicrous.

"No." He dispelled whatever thoughts pulled him under their allure with a small shake of his head. "He appeared to be unwell when I visited him. Highly unlikely for a shifter... he has a cold."

"A cold?" I asked dumbly in a flat tone.

"Yes." He said.

Char gave me "this is a very important info" type of a slow nod when I turned my gaping mouth to her.

"I'm still sleeping, aren't I?" With a slightly unhinged giggle I jerked back in my seat and dropped the almost empty mug on the side table with a clink. "It would explain why all of you are acting so out of character, as well as all the crazy that my brain is trying to conjure into reality disguised as a dream."

Both of them made no comment. They did watch me with concern though, but I didn't care.

"I think that we need to look into the attack in the store and see what is going on." Char said conversationally after watching me for a while. "I trust my instinct and this screams trouble from a mile away. First the hyenas, now a shifter, an alpha on top of that is sick with a cold like a mortal. I have a couple of contacts in Louisiana I can reach out to and see what I can dig out on these witches."

"While you're at it, you promised me lots of coffee." I wiggled the empty mug at her after gulping whatever was left without taking a breath. The headache was gone and it only actuated my need for caffeine more.

"Is she always like this?" Dimitri turned to my bestie, talking about me like I wasn't there.

"Yes." Char and I said at the same time.

"Every morning when she wakes up." Char rolled her eyes but did get off her butt and took the empty mug dangling from my fingers to refill it. "If you want her to function like an adult…" she paused on the way to the kitchen to give me a onceover over her shoulder. "Or whatever passes as an adult when it comes to her these days, you need to caffeinate her excessively. Her brain is no longer on standby after the second cup, so don't let her fool you."

The alpha was nodding as if he was taking mental notes about the instruction manual on how to troubleshoot Alaska. I narrowed my eyes on him, which earned me a small smile in return.

It took me a whole minute to realize the weird muffled sound coming from deeper in the apartment was one of my payphones that I used for jobs. Those with less moral grounds, not my candle making. The second it hit me what the chirping was I shot out of the chair like a bullet and rushed to my bedroom to snatch it off the dresser.

"Who is it?" I jumped a foot off the ground when Char spoke from the doorway. How she kept scaring me I had no idea.

"It's a job." I wiggled the phone to show her it was a payphone and my eyebrows hit my hairline when I found Dimitri looming over her shoulder. "You two move in a pair now?"

"What kind of a job?" My friend ignored my jab.

"One that requires my expertise." I kept my eyes on

Char but I could feel Dimitri burning a hole in my head with how hard he was staring at me.

"You're not accepting it." She cut the air between us with a sharp jerk of her hand.

"Really?" The incredulity was so thick in my tone it could be cut with a knife. I never did well with authority and it rubbed me all sorts of wrong when anyone tried to tell me what I could or couldn't do.

Char knew that.

"I don't think you are understanding the gravity of the situation we are in, Allie."

Dimitri wisely stayed silent.

My temper flared.

"Pray do tell what am I missing about it."

"You are just being reckless and stubborn now." With a huff she started tapping her foot. It should've warned me to shut my trap, but it didn't. "There are people, most probably witches, who want you dead, Alaska. You are not taking any jobs until the threat to your life is over."

"I hate to break it to you, Char, but I'm a witch. There was a threat to my life from the day I was born and it'll be there until the day I'm killed or die. It was always present even when we pretended otherwise." All frustration drained from me in a wave when I noticed she was fighting tears and hiding them behind anger. "I'll be okay, Char. I need you to trust me. This is what I do."

"I can't lose you, Allie. You are all I've got." Despite the alpha witnessing our sappy conversation we had a silent one too, one only best friends can have, and ignored his presence.

"You won't. I'll be extra careful, but my reputation is on the line here, Char. I need to accept it unless there is a solid reason for rejecting it. First, I'll research it." Moving closer I took her hand and squeezed her fingers in reassurance. "I'll be fine. Promise."

It looked like she wanted to say more, to maybe argue again in hopes to convince me otherwise. But, Dimitri as usual had to open his mouth and ruin my life for me.

"I'm going with you." The jerk made it an indisputable statement.

"Like hell you are." Was my automatic reply.

"Try and stop me, little witch."

"I'm going, too." Char jumped in and my groan was ripped out of me all the way from my bare, purple painted toes.

That's how I ended up looking at a new thieving job and how to do with an audience.

Chapter Ten

"Remind me again, why did we have to accompany Dimitri to his fiancées parents house?" I fidgeted in the back seat of the alpha's car and muttered under my breath to Char while she pointedly ignored my question.

Granted, I asked it at least a dozen times in the last five minutes and I'm sure her answer of '*to snoop*' hasn't changed, but I was getting antsy. The longer Dimitri spoke on the phone to a guy who was complaining about babysitting a vampire during the day and being bored out of his mind, the more some intuition was firing up alarms in mine.

Everything in me was screaming to turn around and walk away, more so when we entered the pack's grounds than the moment I dumbly listened to Char and got my ass in the car. Deep down I wanted to convince myself that I wanted to stay away from them in case they notice how often I glance in Dimitri's direction; not that I could do anything to control that. The male was a flame and I was the silly moth. It wasn't even a conscious action. One minute I was looking elsewhere the next I'd be locking eyes with him and all the air leaves my lungs.

It was insane.

Just like the very moment I was thinking that and we got locked in a stare-down through the rearview mirror. He didn't even pause in the conversation he was having. His irises flared up though and my belly did a somersault, so I jerked my eyes away and watched through the window unseeing.

It was my mother's journal to blame.

That was it.

Whatever happened the day before crossed some wires inside my brain and I was totally acting out of character. Because who in all the worlds needed Dimitri Bell to destroy a single life? Not me, that was for sure. By all accounts I had a lot of other people gunning for my head and didn't need to add more.

A movement caught my attention from the line of trees hugging the road we were on. It took a bit to realize it was a streak of fur weaving in and out through the foliage and bushes, as the shifter kept pace with us. When I did notice him, a weird sense of suspicion twisted in my belly.

"We have company." I said to no one in particular, and as soon as the words were out two amber eyes locked on me immediately from the outside. "Damn shifters and their hearing." I added on purpose.

"Shit stirrer." Char snorted nervously from the front of the car.

My lips curled at the corners automatically at her comment and I pretended like I didn't notice the humor in Dimitri's gaze when he glanced back at me.

"You know it." I told my bestie, straightening up in the back seat when the large log cabin came into view.

The long driveway opened in a circular path outlined with perfectly manicured shrubbery and rose bushes. Loose red, white and pink petals littered the cement like droplets of spilled blood on the edges.

A shiver raked my spine.

Dragging my eyes away from the flowers I focused on the large flashy fountain that was the centerpiece of the noteworthy lawn. Two wolves were curled around each other standing on the peak of a mountain their snouts raised up in the air as they howled at the moon. It was a very pretty piece, even I could admit that as much as it irked me to do so. I didn't want to like anything connected to the bombshell engaged to Dimitri Bell.

Not even a fountain.

So, when Char's nails dug into the skin on my forearm, I suppressed the surprised shriek by a hair. It took great effort to strangle the sound and let it die in my throat but I proudly managed it. Through watery eyes I stared at my friend who looked as if she's seen a ghost.

"Char?" My croak was met with nblinking eyeballs ready to pop out of my friend's face.

Instead of an answer, her shaking finger stabbed at the air in the direction of the trickling water coming out of the open mouths of the wolves. Dumbly I blinked at the fountain a few times before seeing what she was mutely trying to show me. Between the lips of each wolf a white Calla dangled, its long petals barely grazing the water before it fell.

"What is going on?" Dimitri to his credit didn't so much as turn in case someone would notice something was amiss.

My temper flared and all shock dissipated into nothingness.

"Do Angela's parents decorate with Calla Lilies on a

regular bases or is tonight a special occasion?" Pushing the words through clenched teeth I glared daggers at the back of the alpha's head. "Did you tell anyone that Char and I would be accompanying you here?"

That made the alpha jerk in the driver seat like he got electrocuted. It gave me great satisfaction to unnerve him but at that moment the reaction was unsettling for me, too.

"I told Angela, yes." And just like that he was back to being calm and collected as if nothing was wrong.

"How do you do it?" Pushing aside all the ramifications of me being on pack's land while Calla's dangled to taunt me, I voiced the question circling my mind and kept my gaze on him in hopes to stop the panic attack, which was clawing at my insides. I'd be damned if I let the shifters see me have a meltdown.

"Do what?" He glanced at me for a split second through the rearview mirror but kept his eyes on the road while we rolled slowly forward toward the lined-up valets waiting to park our car.

"Stay so calm in the middle of the shit-show invading our lives?"

Dimitri shook his head at me although one side of his mouth curled up at the corner. Char snorted a nervous laugh but said nothing, instead opting to scan the area around us like it would reveal some secrets to us suddenly while smoothing her floor length black dress in hopes to remove the invisible wrinkles.

"I wish I had your control sometimes." Muttering under my breath I wiped my sweaty palms on the slacks I was wearing, following my friend's lead.

We might have chaos wrecking us inside but that didn't mean we couldn't look presentable and collected on the outside. The silky blouse I had on me, dipped dangerously low at the front where the fabric gathered, and it tickled my skin as I shifted left and right in my seat, reminding me to straighten from my slouch. Its deep emerald color brought out the color of my eyes more, or so Char loved to say, and I didn't argue when she told me to put it on.

No one had ever accused me of being a fashionista.

But, I was digressing and focused back on our surroundings.

"What do you think it could mean?" Char asked under her breath, doing her best not to move her lips. "Apart from the obvious."

"Whoever was hired to decorate was partial to lilies?" Dimitri slowed the car down and waited patiently for the young boy to dart and open the door for him.

Two others, bright eyed and bushytailed, rushed as well yanking the doors open for Char and I.

"I very much doubt that." I forced a smile as I joined Dimitri and Char at the entrance of the mansion and accepted the offered elbow from the alpha. "But, we are here now. Let's mingle with the wolves."

"Behave." Char mumbled as we allowed the alpha to lead us inside the wolves' den.

Literally.

If I expected some extravagance which was more typical for the vamps, truth be told, I would've been very disappointed. Apart from everyone being dressed in their finest, the place looked cozy and intimate. More a family reunion than a socialite party.

"Darling," a woman's sultry purr set my teeth on edge. "You made it."

Angela emerged from the mass of people milling around, and glided over the polished floors toward us with both arms opened wide and her eyes locked on her male. A natural reaction on my part, I tried to tug my arm from the crook of his elbow and step away but the bastard tightened his hold on me.

"Angela." Dimitri offered a sharp nod to his wife-to-be and instead of embracing her as she expected he released Char who had locked arms with him opposite me, and pushed my best friend between them. "You remember Charmaine Marietti, don't you?"

The blonde bombshell skidded to a stop and sharpened her gaze on Char like the predator that she was with a flick of her high ponytail that kept swinging at her back like a pendulum. My friend straightened her shoulders and I braced myself in case she tried reaching inside her tote for some potion which would melt the skin off Angela's face or something. What in the stars was Dimitri thinking using the sorceress as a shield?

Was he trying to get us killed?

"In any case, I'm sure Angela remembers me." In a crazy attempt to avoid a disaster, I yanked my arm away from the alpha none to gently and stepped next to Char so I can face the she-wolf, shoulder to shoulder with my friend.

"We met once." Her bright blue gaze snapped to me and narrowed.

My heart started a staccato rhythm, bouncing off my ribs while I wondered why I wasn't home researching the new job offer instead of accompanying Dimitri to his rendezvous with his lover. Not for the first time I regretted letting them rope me into coming to the party.

"Nice to see you again." Forcing a smile, I stabbed my hand at her for a handshake.

After staring at my hand as if it was a snake and would bite her, Angela took my fingers in hers with a bruising grip and yanked me close enough that her ponytail tickled my nose. "Why are you here?" She hissed in my ear.

"I'm wondering that myself at the moment." I muttered under my breath and with a firm tug extracted my hand from her hold. "Nice party." My drawl earned me another narrowed eyed glare.

"What is the meaning of this, Dimitri?" Pushing all pretenses aside she turned to her male. The anger disappeared and she almost appeared tired. "We had a deal."

"We need to talk." Watching her steadily, the alpha didn't blink an eye at the drastic change in behavior.

Char and I glanced at each other in confusion.

"You have bad timing." Angela collected herself faster than I could blink and smiled seductively at her fiancée. "Right this way." The silky fabric of her silver dress swished around her knees as she spun in place and swaying her hips walked away from us. The crowd parted like the Red Sea in front of her, many eyeing her hungrily.

"Don't go too far." Dimitri told us as he hurried to follow behind her.

"What just happened?" Anger was beginning to churn in my gut at the whole absurdity of the situation when I asked Char through clenched teeth.

"They need to talk," she told me, cool as a cucumber, plucking two flutes of champagne from a passing tray. "We need to snoop." Handing me one of the delicate glasses she sipped gently from hers. "Come, stop acting like some uncivilized beast. We've been invited to enough parties to know how to act in polite society."

"Right." Making sure no eyes were on me I gulped half of the bubbly beverage. "Because it's much smarter to be here when someone is sending assassins to end you, instead of running for your life."

"Exactly." Char threaded arms with mine and guided me through the open double doors further into the mansion. "Everyone would expect us to hide. A party is the last place anyone would look for us."

I wanted to argue but I kept my mouth shut. She had a very good point. No one in their right mind would be going to parties if a life was on the line. But apparently my friend was not done with her perception on our situation.

"Plus, I really wanted to see if any of the you know who would be here." She breathed the sentence from the corner of her mouth before beaming brightly at a shifter who was eyeing her like he would want nothing more but to howl above her instead of at the full moon. "It all started with that job, so I have this nagging feeling that somehow all of it is connected."

Since it took me a moment to understand who she was referring to, I kept sipping from my glass, hiding my frown, while she was making googly eyes at the guy. We parked ourselves at the edge of the overflowing room where we could watch the interactions of everyone for the most part.

I caught myself a few times glancing in the direction Dimitri and Angela went much to my disappointment. It was none of my business what the two of them did. I had other things to worry about. Like the witches that Char was referring to and to see if maybe they were indeed invited to this party as she suspected. Maybe they were connected to both packs.

At that point anything was possible.

Straining to eavesdrop on conversations, I perused the smiling faces, occasionally reaching to snatch finger food from passing trays. To give credit where credit was due, Angela's parents outdid themselves from decorations to the catering. Everything was tasteful and delicious. It could've been the fact that the clock was ticking on my life which made me appreciate the little things but for just a second, I did stop thinking and just enjoyed the moment.

"I'd like to think the expression of pure bliss you have is a result of my wife's excellent taste in wine." A deep voice full of humor had me snapping my eyes open. I had no idea I closed them.

No one had to interduce the older man standing next to me, his tux stretched over wide shoulders big enough to toss a grown male as if he weighed nothing. The light, almost white, blond hair and bright blue eyes were so much like Angela's it was unnerving. The only differences between him and his daughter were, his nose which was a little wider and he had thinner lips.

"It's delicious." I stuttered caught off guard. "Everything is, not just the wine."

The older man smiled brightly at me. Who knew I could be charming.

Not me, that's for sure.

"I think my nephew would agree with that statement when it comes to your friend." He chuckled, pointing with his chin toward the shifter who was striding across the vast room straight for Char.

"You are too kind." My friend giggled like a schoolgirl, batting her eyelashes and dialing up her charm to a thousand.

A sense of urgency rippled through me with such a foreboding feeling I shivered visibly and my heart galloped wildly in my chest. Cold sweat washed over me numbing my entire body. Angela's father noticed and a line formed between his brows as he opened his mouth to, I'm guessing, ask if I was okay.

"Excuse me, I'll be right back. I think I might've had

one too many drinks". I rushed to say before he could utter a word and with a tight smile hurried away from him and Char.

Thankfully, my friend recovered quickly and started talking to the older man to divert his attention from me just as the young shifter reached our side of the room. She might be upset that I left her to deal with them on her own and I'd probably hear a lot about it but I had to get away from the crowd before I fainted. With one last glance I darted into the hallway and away from them in search of a bathroom. I needed a place to breathe for a second before I turned myself invisible.

Something was not right inside Angela's home, and I needed to find out what hopefully before it was too late.

Chapter Eleven

"*À sealladh,*" I muttered and watched my reflection slowly disappear from the mirror in the bathroom. After a few deep breaths and with the safety of my powers I was ready to go face whatever sent a wave of warning to me earlier in the evening.

There was no mistaking it. Something, or someone, wanted my attention.

Well, they had it.

The sound of hundreds of voices assaulted my ears when I nudged the door open, praying that no one would be on the other side. It would've been a lot of fun trying to explain that one to a half-drunk shifter or worse a vamp. A few of the bloodsuckers were milling around that I noticed along with elementals and mages. Anyone that was someone in LA was invited that night. Luckily for me, the hallway was empty and all the partygoers were too busy drinking, eating, and chatting to care what I was doing.

Acid was burning the inside of my stomach from the apprehension riding me hard ever since that strange feeling lit a fire under my butt, so I pressed my hand on my belly in hopes to calm it down.

Now that no one could see me I had time to stop and focus on my intuition, too. There was no doubt it'd lead me to where I had to go if I wasn't too distracted with other things. With one ear on my surroundings in case a person bumped into me while I wasn't watching, I opened to the magic tentatively.

The lavish home bloomed behind my closed eyelids, the auras from everyone present pulsing with their individual vibrations and connecting to each other with a thin intertwined thread. It twisted and turned forming a web of pulsing points with me in the center. It was so beautiful it brought tears to my eyes until I felt a tug on my subconscious, gentle at first but more urgent with each passing breath.

I followed it.

Heart beating wildly and eyes at half mist I walked through the large home admiring the artwork and statues strategically placed all over the place. My fingers grazed the wall on one side, and I offered smiles to the staff I passed knowing too well that they couldn't see me. There was something liberating in the fact that no matter what I do I could not be seen.

The feeling led me to the other side of the mansion, and I stopped dead in my tracks in front of a closed door.

It looked like it could be an office.

Or a broom closet for all I cared.

My predicament was clear. I had to open the door to see what was on the other side but how to do it without bringing attention to my invisible ass lurking like a specter through the hallways? The answer came around the corner, with unassuming features, her golden ponytail swishing behind her as she hurried past me carrying a large tray of drinks. Reaching over, I flicked one of the glasses off the silver platter and the young woman gasped when it shattered on the floor, splashing its contents over both our feet.

I stepped away from her line of sight and the moment she lowered her burden and leaned down to pick up the larger pieces of glass with a groan, I grabbed the door handle and pushed it open a sliver. The woman raised her head with a frown but continued to collect what she could from the mess I made, muttering under her breath about not being paid enough to deal with crap like this.

Making a valiant effort not to make a sound, I tiptoed toward the slightly open door and froze in my tracks when it was yanked open all the way and a furious Angela filled the doorway, rage burning bright in her eyes. The light coming from behind her made her dress appear like liquid silver that was emerging through her skin to hug the parts of her body she didn't want revealed and her hair looked almost white. If I didn't know she was a shifter, and she didn't have curves to prove that little fact, I would've mistaken her for a Fae. She sure had the height to be one, high heeled sandals aside.

"What do you want?" Gone was the husky, seductive tone she normally used on Dimitri when she snapped at the still kneeling woman.

"Umm, I'm...," the poor lady stuttered, blinking owlishly at Angela. "I'm so sorry, I..." she glanced helplessly at the mess around her and dejectedly just lifted the pieces of glass to show what she was doing.

I felt like the biggest ass on the planet.

"Why did you open the door?" Angela showed no sympathy toward the woman who appeared to wish the ground would swallow her. "Did you open it?" With that question the she-wolf stepped out into the hallway and looked up and down to check if anyone else was there.

Taking the chance I'd been given, I darted around her and into the room. I could hear the two women talking but their voices faded into the background when I lifted my head and locked eyes with Dimitri. He stood in front of a large window in what turned out to be an office and not a broom closet, half way turned toward the door as if I caught him midturn. I knew he couldn't see me but the way he had his gaze locked on mine immediately could've fooled me for sure.

I blinked and whatever spell he had me under broke, returning sound with it. I had to put some effort into figuring out the weird connection I felt with the alpha because it was not just insane but also unhealthy. However, now was neither the time nor the place for my personal shortcomings.

"The door must not have been properly closed, Miss." The lady was saying to Angela. "It cracked open when I stepped closer to pick up the broken glass so no one would step on it by accident."

"How convenient for you." The she wolf spat with disgust. And to my shock, grabbed the woman by the collar of her shirt lifting her to dangle on her tiptoes. All that in needle thin heels mind you so I made a mental note to never piss Angela off. "Who do you work for, huh? Who sent you to eavesdrop?"

"No...no one...please. No one sent me." the poor human, and there was no doubt that she was human by the way she started sweating and shaking, squeaked first from surprise then from fear. "I was carrying drinks from the kitchen. I don't even work for the catering company full time. I'm paid by the hour when I do accept a job. Paid poorly, too, if my life is threatened like this."

"Angela," Dimitri finally got involved, gaining his wife-to-be's attention. "Let the woman go. I'm sure she didn't mean to open the door. We were in such a rush I'm sure we didn't close it properly." In a few long strides he was next to Angela, his hand pressed to the small of her back. "Besides, we are engaged. It doesn't matter who can hear us." The pointed look suggested they were doing a lot of things while the door was closed but talking was not one of them.

The acid that finally settled in my stomach decided to start churning again so I looked away. What in the stars was the matter with me? Gnawing on the side of my thumb I tried to focus on the room while praying I won't see discarded panties, or a condom. That would've taught me a lesson on snooping around.

"God no." The woman recoiled as if insulted. "I heard nothing, I swear. There was not a sound coming from anywhere until the door fully opened."

"See?" The alpha chuckled. "We were discrete, after all."

He reached and extracted the woman's shirt from Angela's grip while both women were watching him as if he mysteriously appeared in front of them. It was a little unnerving the effect he had on the female population.

"I apologize for my fiancée." Dimitri continued with light conversation as if the poor human didn't nearly swallow her tongue out of fear. "She detests gossip, you see. I'm sure you understand the importance of secrecy. Yes?" Opening his suit jacket he pulled out a wad of cash, by the looks of it all one hundred-dollar bills, and handed it to the gaping woman. "For your discretion, and as a way of an apology. Please."

The lady all but forgot to be freaked out when she saw the Benjamins. She was nodding excitedly like a bobble head, hugging the cash to her chest. I found myself gliding closer to the door where they were all standing, ready to reach my hand out and remind the alpha I was here too and he needed to pay up if he wanted me to keep my trap shut as well. Fortunately, I caught myself in time before doing something stupid like that. I'm sure Char would have a field day when I told her about it.

"Thank you." Dimitri smiled at the woman and she would've dived for him if Angela didn't pin her with a glare.

"My pleasure." The blond bobbed her head a couple more times and darted away leaving the tray and the broken glass forgotten in the hallway.

"That would've been a disaster." Dimitri made a point of closing the door soundly while I stood frozen staring at the two of them like a creep.

"What if she heard something?" Angela dropped the act of a feral beast and began wringing her hands in distress.

"She didn't." The alpha tucked one hand in the pocket of his pants while raking the fingers of the other through his hair. "She didn't lie when she said she wasn't sent to eavesdrop. I would've smelled a lie, and so would you."

"Unless she was compelled to believe she wasn't sent to overhear something." Angela wasn't backing down and I found myself inching closer. "There must be a reason why half of the house is full of vampires. There are things you don't even know that have been going on. I fear I don't even know everything that's going on despite all my efforts to stay informed."

"As I was saying before this whole charade," he shook his head on a sigh, "that would be too much effort to simply confirm we are a couple, Angela. Let's be reasonable."

"We are talking ancient prophecies here, Dimitri. People die to protect them, and…" Spinning on her heel she sashayed toward the mini bar at the edge of the office. "…some will go to great lengths to ensure what was written will come to pass. Never doubt that."

"I never disagreed nor did I dispute any of the prophecies." Tucking his other hand in the pocket as well, the alpha rocked back on his heels. "All I'm saying is, we can't afford to start getting paranoid. If we look for enemies around every corner, I'm sure we would find them."

"They are around every corner." After filling a glass with straight scotch, she turned to face him and tossed it back until half of it was empty. "That's strong." The she wolf coughed, and blinked fast to dispel the tears gathering in her eyes.

"As it should be." Dimitri walked over and took the drink from her fingers. "We have a solid plan, Angela. We need to stick to it."

"You don't say." Drawling, the blonde squinted at him. "It was not me that brought the two females here, now was it? What were you thinking?"

"I told you what I was thinking." Calm and collected as always, he took a sip of the scotch and watched her for a long moment over the rim of the glass. "Someone is trying to remove one or both of them from the face of the earth and everything tells me it's connected with this…With me."

"You honestly think they are part of the prophecy?" All color drained from her face and she held her breath for the answer.

"Indubitably."

"You think she is the one on your tattoo?" Angela's hand rose up as if to touch him but she thought better of it and let it drop to her side. "What a mess."

"It's only a mess if we allow it to be."

"It's not like I wanted this." She stepped around him so she could pace the office, wearing a track in the thick, blood-colored rug. "My father did this without my agreement too. But I came to terms with it. You should, as well. For all our sakes."

"I have it under control." Dimitri muttered under his breath and at the same moment turned to look over his shoulder straight at me.

My heart stopped before rattling raucously in my chest.

"I hope so." Angela was about to say something else since her lungs filled with air but she was left with her lips parted and her hand halfway raised toward the alpha when the door burst open and Char rushed in followed by Angela's father.

"We have a problem." My bestie gasped, hanging onto the door handle like it was the only thing holding her up. She must've been running.

I almost gave myself away when I tensed to go help her but Dimitri beat me to it. Thank the stars.

"What's wrong?" Angela hurried to her father, concern etched on her pretty face.

"A pack of hyenas is circling the premises with a full nest of feral vampires. They are on something, Dimitri. None of them are responding to anyone including the elders of their kind who were invited here." The old alpha faced his soon to be son-in-law. "We have a house full of people, most that haven't seen a problem they couldn't fix by throwing money at it."

"We must find Alaska." Char ignored everything that was said and my heart warmed from how much she cared about me. "Like now. I don't care if the damn hyenas start gnawing on guests like they've found chew toys, you are helping me find my friend first, wolf."

"Come, Miss Marietti," Dimitri left Angela and her father gaping at him when he took Char by the upper arm and strode out the open door. "I think I know where your friend might be." He glanced back as if saying *you better be there before us, Alaska.*

I tiptoed after them without a second thought.

Chapter Twelve

"She's not here." Char was turning frantically this way and that at the top of the wide staircase, the long skirts of her dress swishing around her ankles. "Allie?" She whisper-yelled loud enough every supernatural in the mansion to hear her. "Alaska McCullough, get over here this instant."

"Stop getting everyone's attention, she...," Dimitri was saying when I finally reached them, barely able to keep myself from panting loudly since I had to jog up the damn stairs.

"I'm here." I told them and draped myself over the railing of the last couple of steps so I could catch my breath. "Seriously, did you have to come up here, Dimitri? I'm aware that you don't like me. There is absolutely no need to prove it by trying to kill me like this."

Char on the other hand had a different problem it seemed because she totally ignored my whining. "You can see her?" she hissed at the alpha then rounded on me or where she assumed I would be. "He can see you, and I can't?"

"No." We both answered her although mine was more of a question than stating a fact.

My friend narrowed her eyes not being convinced for a second that we were telling her the truth. I couldn't blame her. I didn't believe the wolf either that he couldn't see me. People were speaking with loud voices downstairs however, all gathering around the tall windows to watch what was happening outside. If Dimitri could see through my magic or not would have to wait.

"Hang on." Pushing off the railing I rushed into the nearest open door and dispersed the spell so I could actually talk without worrying if anyone could hear me. "We need to get out of here before someone gets hurt." I told them as I returned to join them at the top of the stairs.

"You should've stayed invisible, Allie, if that was your plan." Char pointed out the obvious. Her foot started tapping too which was never a good sign.

"And let someone else suffer because whoever is outside is looking for me but can't find me?" With a snort, I leaned over the railing in hopes to see if anything had changed downstairs with a hand pressed to the center of my chest so my boobs don't pop out uninvited. "That's not happening, Char. If they want me, they'll need to catch me first."

"I'm not sure they'll see that as the challenge you want it to be." My heart skipped a beat when Angela spoke from behind us. "Something is seriously wrong with the vampires and hyenas outside. Come," she spun on her heel and walked away without worry if we would follow or not.

Of course, all three of us took the bait and followed silently down another hallway with a plush runner stretched from one end to the other at the very center of the gleaming parquet. As we walked, I glanced at Dimitri from the corner of my eye in case I could see any indication he was expecting Angela, but I caught him openly studying me instead.

"What?" I mouthed so I don't provoke the she wolf in any way.

He grinned.

An honest to goodness grin that scrambled my brain when it lit up his face and popped those dimples out. I stared dumbfounded and didn't realize Char stopped walking so I collided with her back, bounced off her, and ended up on my butt with a grunt.

"Shit." Char gasped reaching for me. "Are you okay?"

Blowing the few strands of hair that fell over my face with a huff I gave her a deadpan look. What kind of a question was it, are you okay, when she sees me sprawled down at her feet like some prostrated peasant?

"Come look." Angela's voice came from an open doorway so I took Char's offered hand and pretended I didn't notice Dimitri didn't try help.

I did debate tripping him when he walked around us to enter the room, though. The moment we followed I wished we stayed out in the hallway ignorant of what was out to get us. Honestly, there had to be a moment in one's life where the universe, Fates or whoever was in charge said you know what? This person has had enough, we should cut this one some slack.

"What in the stars is that?" I physically shrunk back from the scene down on the manicured lawn.

Everything made sense. Why Angela's father looked so worried and why no one dared to step a foot outside of the mansion. It was eerie and unnerving to a point it was eliciting physical reactions from all of us. Even Dimitri shivered when we stepped in front of the wall made out of glass.

Lined up in two rows with a precision of an architect,

vampires surrounded the house. They stood stock still, arms loosely hanging by their sides, heads bowed down like they were asleep standing up. Next to each vampire sat a hyena tongue lolling to the side, black holes instead of eyes in their gaunt faces.

What alarmed me the most was the moment I stepped next to the floor to ceiling window all of the vampires heads snapped up and their eyes locked on me. The hyenas jerked to attention too, their empty eye sockets lighting up with blood red irises, which glowed unnaturally in their faces. Cold sweat washed over me and fear numbed my entire body.

"They are spelled." Char moved close to me, her shoulder brushed mine when she pressed her hand on the glass. "Witch magic." She turned to face me, her face blank of any emotion.

"Did you tell anyone we were coming tonight, Angela?" I asked the question but kept my eyes locked on my friend. I could see the fear and turmoil churning behind the calm way she gazed at me. Dimitri was being unusually silent but it suited me just fine. Hopefully I could forget he was even there.

"Why would I do that?" The bombshell sounded genuinely perplexed glancing between all three of us as to why I would think we were important enough for her to mention.

"I thought the decorations on the fountain in the front yard were quite interesting." When Angela frowned at me probably wondering if I had lost my mind I hurried to come up with some explanation to my comment. "The flowers are Char's favorite. It's not exactly the season for Calla Lilies, so I assumed..."

"You don't know what you are talking about." She

sounded oddly upset that I would dare comment on the decorations. Or so I thought at first. "My father built that fountain for my mother when they lost their first pup at childbirth. He will rip the throat of anyone out, including me, if someone goes anywhere near it. If you didn't imagine the flowers we have a much bigger problem than the spelled shifters and vampires."

"The flowers were there." Dimitri spoke barely above whisper. "I saw them as well."

"Stay here. I'll be back." Angela didn't need more convincing. She practically sprinted out of the room leaving a cloud of some musky perfume in her wake.

"Allie." Char bumped me with her shoulder to get my attention. I dragged my eyes from the spot Angela was occupying not long ago to my friend. "Do you think they may have a seer working for them? It could explain how they know where to corner us every time." Her unsmiling face turned from me to the alpha and back. "Maybe that's why we play catch up. They are always one step ahead."

"That's ludicrous, Char. You know it as well as I do." I dismissed the idea immediately. "It's impossible to find a seer worth half the effort you need to protect her. It's like finding a unicorn if you discover one who could see the future for real."

"As impossible as finding a Louisiana coven of witches migrating to LA?" Char cocked an eyebrow at me, looking unimpressed.

My mouth opened, then closed.

"It is as unfeasible as finding a witch in Santa Monica, passing for a candlemaker." Dimitri finished hammering the point with a smirk on his face.

"Okay, fine. I admit I could be wrong. Make sure you mark the day in your calendar, Char." Blowing out an annoyed breath I turned to look down at the creeps outside. "Probable? Not likely. Possible? Maybe."

"Be that as it may, we must proceed as we planned. This changes nothing apart from having us be more prepared." The alpha said it like someone died and made him God.

He even stretched his neck a bit to look over both our heads out the window with such an apathic expression you'd think the spelled souls outside inconvenienced his Sunday brunch.

"Why are we hanging out with this guy again?" I tilted my head closer to Char and muttered in a low tone as if he won't hear me. "He seriously thinks he can boss us around. Look at him." My elbow jabbed into her ribs and she flinched away. "Just look."

"Play nice with the wolf, Allie." Char snorted at the frown bunching up Dimitri's forehead. "We might need his help sooner than you think."

"I dunno. I doubt he knows how to play fetch." Try as I could I wasn't able to hide the humor from my tone.

Pressing both hands on the glass, I leaned into it straining my neck to see up but it was difficult. While we talked and waited on Angela, I scanned the area outside and was pleased to see the pack had woods almost attached to the back of the mansion, the tall trees stretching their branches to brush parts of the large home on one corner. That could work to our advantage if I could figure out how to get up on the roof.

"How many stories is this house?" Looking over my shoulder I nearly touched Dimitri's chest with my nose. I didn't notice when he moved that close to me. "I see you still haven't learned about personal space."

Storm blue eyes lazily blinked down at me while the alpha totally ignored me as if I had not spoken. My heart picked up speed and I was grateful for the coolness of the glass or the chances were I would've turned into a puddle right there and then. When his nostrils flared his gaze sharpened on my face.

"Three stories," Dimitri answered. "Plus, the basement and attic, which are counted as a double level each." At my raised eyebrow he shrugged slightly. "The pack uses the house as their headquarters. They need the space."

"I think I have an idea on how we can get the hyenas and vamps out of here where we don't have to worry about me being seen where I'm using my…you know." Wiggling my fingers in the air to indicate my magic I leaned into the glass again to make sure that one tree I had been eyeing would work. "I do need a rope though. So, that might be a slight problem. I didn't exactly come prepared to crawl up buildings from the outside."

"Ropes are not a problem." Angela joined the conversation again as if she never left. "My parents developed a love for rock climbing, we have enough equipment for an army here somewhere."

The curvy wolf sauntered into the room completely unclothed, and my friend and the alpha didn't blink an eye at all the exposed skin she was flaunting. In her hand she carried a bouquet of dripping wet Calla Lilies, which she unceremoniously tossed onto the sleek cream rug at our feet. Her hair was loose too, falling like a silky waterfall over her shoulders and down her back. Char and Dimitri were unfazed since every normal person knew nudity amongst shifters was commonplace, but my eyes remained fixated on the unexpected sight a second too long to be considered polite.

I felt like a creep.

Not wanting for the female to catch me staring like a

teenage boy that had never seen boobs before, I pointed at the Callas on the floor. It was discernable this close that they were not of the magical variety, thank the stars. They looked real enough before, but I didn't want to keep looking at them to remind myself why they were placed on the fountain in the first place.

"They were not worth your life if any of the shifters or vamps attacked." I told Angela but she only blinked at me like I'd spoken a foreign language.

"The alternative was my father going feral, and in his state killing a bunch of his associates." Nodding in gratitude she took the jacket Dimitri offered her and she slipped it on, finally covering up her nudity. "Which is never good for business…or so I've heard." The female snorted making me think I missed some inside joke somewhere.

"Judging by the uninvited guests we have I'm guessing your ex was a bloodsucker?" Angela turned to Char this time with an expression full of understanding. "They do tend to get very possessive like this." Her hand twirled in the direction of the flowers.

It took me a moment to realize that Angela thought an ex-lover of Char's was trying to win her over since I dumbly said Callas were my friend's favorite flowers. It was much better than the alternative of me confessing who and what I was by any stretch so I didn't correct her.

"You should not have gone outside alone, Angela." Dimitri scowled like some grandfather. "We don't know what we are dealing with."

"Don't we?" Cocking a hip she didn't back down which elevated her in my book. "It's obvious it's some potion gone wrong that they took. Maybe the dude thought she would feel empathy for them and try to fix it. She is a sorceress after all, isn't she?"

The conversation was taking us nowhere, and we were running out of time; I could feel it in my bones. The psycho hive mind creatures outside weren't going to stay transfixed for much longer my intuition warned me.

"About the rock-climbing equipment that you mentioned." I chirped in, batting my eyelashes at the she wolf who looked as if she forgot I was there. I was not sure if I should be offended. "Can we get it now? Sooner rather than later would be preferred."

"And what are you planning on doing with it, may I ask?" Bright blue eyes narrowed down on me as if I was a five-year-old asking to play with the expensive china. "Throw candles at the bloodsuckers?"

Lots of snarky comments popped in my head many not appropriate to be said on a pirate ship much less in front of people I didn't know too well so I swallowed them down.

"Go out that window so I can try and lead them away from the house." I answered truthfully. "I'll climb."

"*WE* will climb." Char saddled closer to me so she could step on my toes. My eyes crossed from the sharp pain and I bit my tongue to stop myself from screeching. "They were sent after me so I'll lure them away and no one will get hurt."

I decided in that moment that I must be cursed.

There was no other explanation why I had to go through all the insanity in my life.

Chapter Thirteen

"You are the one who insisted on climbing with me." I told Char for the second time not even pretending that I wasn't grinning like a fool. Actually, my cheeks hurt from how hard my mouth was stretched. I was moon-bathing my molars, with how wide I was smiling.

"I didn't plan on showing my good panties to a bunch of drugged up vamps and hyenas when I decided not to let you go alone." Char huffed, blowing upward a corkscrew of hair that had fallen over her eye. She lifted her face to look up at me. "A, thank you for having my back Char, would do instead of that shit eating grin."

"Thank you for having my back, Char." I parroted still smiling when I looked down toward her and almost lost the grip on my rope when I noticed a crowed gathered right under us. "Oh shit." My hand slipped and I clawed at the rope until I snatched it in a white-knuckled grip.

"See what I mean?" My friend rolled her eyes like I was the one doing something unusual. Why wasn't she worried? "I think they are not under a spell but pretending. I could've sworn that vamp," she released her rope with one hand so she could twist around. "That one, the one in the red tank top." Her finger wiggled in the direction she spotted the vampire. "He was gawking up my dress. On purpose."

"Char, I think we should worry that all of them are right under us and could start climbing to kill us. Not that they can see your lace panties," I chided and sped up my climb because I wanted to be away from the spelled creatures.

"They've been there since we stepped out the window and you hooked our ropes to the roof." She followed suit, the skirts of her dress swaying bellow her. "If you paid attention you would've known."

"We are almost there." Stepping to the side, I reached down and offered her a hand.

My toes were gripping the edge of the brick and gave me enough leverage to be able to pull her up. We were almost at the roof where we would flip over and get out of the open, so the sooner we both were at the same height the better.

"Do you think he really was looking at my ass?" She took my hand and pushed as hard as she could to help me bring her higher.

"Why do you care?" Grabbing a hold of the decorative trim and locking my fingers through the holes in it, I hefted myself up and flopped over on the rooftiles. "It is a nice ass. Can you blame him."

"Thank you, Allie. I think it's a nice one too." Her head popped up above the rooftiles. "At least Dimitri has eyes only for you, or I would've freaked out that I showed him my flashy globes, too."

If my eyes opened any wider they would've rolled off of my face and off the roof for the hyenas to gnaw on them.

"Oh, how cute." Char's husky chortle irked me. "You didn't see him craning his neck the entire time?"

Sure as hell when I scrambled to lean over and look, my gaze locked on a glowy blue one. He held me locked for a long moment and with a nod he disappeared inside.

"If you're done making googly eyes I could use a hand." Char groaned from the attempt to pull herself up.

"Sorry." My mumbled apology earned me another groan but I did grab her under her arms and yanked with everything in me. She pushed with her toes on the bricks at the same time and we both toppled over backward, Char dropping like a rock on top of me.

"Holy crap you are…" I wheezed and cut off when her head whipped around, long corkscrews flying, and she pinned me with a glare. "Light as a feather." I finished breathlessly, gasping for air.

"Thanks, it must be all the running for our lives I've done lately. It does wonders for your waistline, you should try it."

"Wonder where all that sass is coming from." I muttered making her snort. "Watch that tile next to your right foot, it shifts if you put too much pressure on it."

Char's phone chirped, so she dove with both hands inside her tote which she obviously brought with her. One of these days I was going to convince her to get me one of them, as well. I had no doubt you could pack a house in it and it won't feel like you are carrying anything rather than a regular purse. It was a bottomless hole full of useful gadgets that had saved our lives on more than one occasion.

"Dimitri says we are all clear." But she was frowning at the phone screen too long for my liking before she tucked it away.

"And?"

"And what?"

"What else did he say?"

"Not to leave pack land without him." Char rolled her eyes. If we kept it up I was pretty sure they would eventually roll off our heads. "I swear sometimes I'm thinking he has never met you, Allie."

"I'm not that bad." Was my automatic reply as I started inching down the roof toward the large tree I was hoping would be our salvation. "You know as well as I do that leaving pack lands so these zombified creatures can follow us and not hurt innocents is the right thing to do."

"Aha. Or you would've totally listened to the wolf's orders." She told me evenly, her faked innocence pushing me to stiffen up and act defensively.

"What would you have me do?" Pausing for a moment I stretched as far as I could so I can look down on the ground. All of them were there, following mutely like zombies. Now that I compared them to the brain eating undead I couldn't stop thinking about them like that. "I have this feeling that whatever spell was used it has a timer or a trigger, Char. We are seriously running out of time."

A strong wind whipped across the trees at the back of the mansion and it whistled through the leaves and branches with an eerie high-pitched sound. We had to crouch and hold into the rooftiles so it doesn't fling us off the roof like kites. The hyenas became animated right after and shrieked from bellow, a few of them laughing in an unhinged and unsettling way. Ghostly hands ran their fingers up and down my spine and gooseflesh pebbled my skin.

I shivered.

"I think you are right". Char whispered from behind me, fear making her voice shake.

"Okay, here is my plan". Waddling sideways I turned to face her. "I was going to use the trees to lead them as deep into the forest as I could before pelting them with every spell I know and hoping they'd die. Or pass out at worst case. But now that you are with me I'm thinking we could slide down a trunk, bolt for the parked cars, and use one of the vehicles to make an escape."

"I came prepared, Allie." She dipped her hand in the tote without looking and pulled it out with three glass jars filled with oily liquid in various colors; all of them clear indicators that whatever was inside was poisonous.

I shrank back which made Char grin like a fiend. "We can still use the trees to take them deeper into the woods as you wanted and then all bets are off. I'll melt the skin off their bones."

"Sometimes you scare me." I admitted but smiled to soften the harsh comment. "I am very grateful you are on my side though."

"I have one here somewhere that can knock out the wolf too if he starts giving you hard time. It'll give him a killer headache for a few days too."

"I thought you two were as thick as thieves now." Spinning around I started crawling on all fours toward the closest branches which were brushing the roof with their wide leaves. Some type of moss was growing around the foliage, too and it draped like grapes in irregular intervals. For just a moment I considered it for maybe using it as a weapon but I changed my mind. As gruesome as it sounded, Char's idea of melting their skins was the safer bet for us.

"I still don't understand why witches would want to kill me." I voiced the one thing that truly bothered me since that morning when the lady came to the store and started asking about love candles. "Dimitri's father, I can understand and even justify to some point. Even Dimitri himself since he is a member of the MPO, if he decided one day that he wants to kill me. But a coven from Louisiana? What in the stars have I done to them?"

Char listened quietly and at that point we reached the thick branches which were reaching over the roof for us like crooked giant hands. The sky had cleared out and the moon hung heavy like a juicy plum suspended in the air. An electric blue ring pulsed around the diameter giving it an otherworldly appearance like some ominous omen dangling above our heads.

Like we needed some more bad signs.

"It doesn't make sense to me either, which is why I initially thought we should stay focused on Dimitri's father. But now looking at the situation, I'm wondering if his so called cold is somehow connected to the zombified version as you call it of vamps and shifters we are dealing with here."

"I overheard Dimitri and Angela talking." I admitted quietly as if afraid he might hear me voice it out loud. "He admitted to her that he believes we are, …, well that I am somehow connected to some old prophecy the wolves have. Because why not, right? Why not add an ancient prophecy to all this shit-show?"

"That does sound like bad news." The sorceress sounded thoughtful, her tone almost absentminded. "Did they say what kind of prophecy?"

"No, but Angela was really worked up about it." Standing up I took hold of the branch and pulled myself up on it, making sure my body was still somewhat visible so the creeps bellow could see me. "I think that same prophecy has everything to do with their soon to be wedding, too. I wish I could say I heard more about it, but I didn't."

We were hiding more from the victims who were cowering inside the house than the assailants who so far were appearing docile. Char followed behind me without complaint, more at home dangling from branches than the rope attached to the house.

"And before you accuse me of doing something so that Dimitri can see through my magic I assure you he can't. But he can somehow sense me when I'm around him even if I'm invisible." I didn't need to tell her how upset that made me. I was livid I couldn't sneak up on him. "I think he can smell me." That last bit was more a reminder for myself than her.

"That's inconvenient." My friend muttered so I stopped moving to look back at her. "What? I can be reasonable."

"Could've fooled me." I quipped and we both chuckled.

"Something is going on down there." The urgency in her tone had me craning my neck as far as I could go to see the ground.

We just entered the tree line lining the property where the trees were starting to thicken and I was grateful for it. As Char mentioned that something was off, all hell broke loose. The hyenas were shaking their heads harshly enough to be unable to walk so they started dropping on their sides and screeching so loud the vamps covered their ears with both hands. At first, I truly believed that it was all the shrieking that was forcing the bloodsuckers to drop on their knees since they were known for their supernatural hearing more so than the shifters. But after a closer inspection I realized it was a sound. A faint one but noticeable to be sure.

Almost like a training dog whistle.

"Do you hear that?" Not wanting to waste more time I started picking up speed and grabbing on to thicker branches that could easily hold my weight. The universe should bless the pack for wanting forests around them. It very well might save our lives.

"You could hear it, too? I thought my ears were ringing." Char huffed but kept pace with me.

"I have a very bad feeling about this, Char."

I should've kept my mouth shut. For some reason whenever I voiced something horrible, it was as if I spoke it into existence. It always happened.

"You had to say it, didn't you." Char knowing my damn luck groaned as if in pain.

The sound stopped and a shout of rage echoed from the creatures below us. Their bellow bounced off the tree trunks when they jerked their heads up and started climbing with breakneck speed.

Chapter Fourteen

"You know, Allie. Sometimes," grunting from the force she put behind her throw Char tossed a glass potion toward a large oak half a yard away from us, exploding it into pieces. "It's better to keep your mouth shut so you don't provoke the Fates. I believe I have brought that to your attention before. Correct?" A dozen or so vampires and hyenas exploded along with it, their body parts flying in all directions.

"You have mentioned it once or twice. Yes." Admitting begrudgingly, I flinched when a broken branch zipped passed my head and embedded itself in the trunk next to my ear. "Char, I love you and would like nothing more than to chat but can we talk about this a bit later, please? I'm little busy trying not to get decapitated here."

As if invited by my snarky comment, a dagger sang through the air, the blade whispering loudly from the speed it was thrown with. My right hand sprang in front of me on reflex, palm facing ahead, and my skin begun to tingle in preparation of the spell.

"*Reothadh.*" Freeze I commanded under my breath and the tip of the long knife touched the center of my palm before it stopped its trajectory. Discarding it with a flick of a wrist I waddled down the branch where I was crouched in hopes to avoid more sharp objects being thrown my way by hiding my body between the leaves as much as possible.

I was a thief damn it, not an action hero. Good at lurking in the shadows and running away, not fighting.

Thank the lucky stars for Char.

The sorceress was a force to be reckoned with, perched on a branch like a falcon with a line etched between her brows and her corkscrew hair wild around her face as she picked her victims off with an unnerving precision.

She'd dip a hand in her tote, lob a potion at someone below us that would be too close for comfort, then mutter something about needing to make more protection charms before pitching another potion at someone's head.

A hyena snickered crazily from below the tree we were using as our standing ground. As much as it bothered me I reached deep within me and pulled on the air magic I stole from the elemental not that long ago. It rushed eagerly under my skin like a cat craving attention and a tremor of unease rushed through me.

"*Thig adhair, dèan mar a tha mi ag àithneadh.*" Come Air, do as I command. I urged the element, hoping to avoid unnecessary deaths of which we already had too many in just that patch of the woods.

Not that I had any problem with any of those wishing me harm dying, per se. I strived to be and considered myself a kind person. Not a saint. The moment they point their sharp blades or powers in my direction I'm done caring for their wellbeing. If they do the same to those I care about I hoped they met their maker in the most painful way possible.

Strong winds picked up through the trees, gaining speed as they neared our little standoff patch. I couldn't tell how many of the attackers we started with but there were a little over a dozen left at that moment when a whirl of air started lifting them off the forest floor along with leaves, rocks and who knows what else.

"Ohhh, smart." Char turned to the side so she could face me and grinned. Only her teeth were visible, unnaturally white, in the moonlight and the glow of the fluorescent potions she flung around at the shifters and vamps. "I could get used to this. Although you should've used it earlier to help us out of the house instead of making me dangle on a rope and show my ass like it's an exhibit A. The vamps were eyeing my white buns. I know it."

"Seriously, Char. You're still stuck on that?"

"I'm not lying you daft woman." Huffing in annoyance she blew a strand of hair out of her face. "My ass cheeks were tingling. I could feel their gazes there."

My mouth opened but nothing came out. We stood untouched in an invisible bubble on our tree while all around us thick branches were swaying harshly left and right, some of them bending down to sweep the forest floor. Vamps and hyenas were clutching the thickest roots for dear life so they don't get lifted in the air. Through the thundering of the strong winds around the trees a howl of a pack of wolves could be heard and goosebumps pebbled my skin freezing anything I was about to say in my throat. It was getting louder, rising over the screaming whirlwinds telling us they were getting closer at an alarming rate. My panicked gaze found Char's and I froze for a long moment not knowing what to do.

"Keep it going." Char yanked her tote in her lap and started rummaging through it frantically. "I have to have something here to explain the winds. I'll find it, you keep going."

Cold sweat trickled down my back while I held the air under my control, pushing harder so I could pick up our attackers and chuck them as far away from us as possible. Maybe we could run back toward the mansion, steal Dimitri's car and get the hell out of there before any of the pack see what was going on here. Fear clawed at my throat tightening my airways like a fist. So lost in all the different scenarios on how my secret would be revealed I didn't notice anyone sneaking up until it was too late. Hand still up in the air so I don't lose connection with the element, I braced myself on the branch and took a deep breath so I would give more effort. That's when I felt it.

The penetrating gaze had a tangible weight to it.

My eyes snapped down, where the roots of our tree were curled up like a barbwire fence to protect us thanks to one of Char's potions. A gray wolf with a wide white patch of fur on his chest stood firm, all his four paws planted on solid soil in the middle of the vortex I was creating like it was a gentle breeze. It struck me as odd not just the fact that it was unaffected by my magic, but that I immediately thought of the wolf as a he instead of a she, yet, there was such certainty about it I could've placed my life on the line if need be.

Without realizing what I was doing, my palm begun lowering and the strong winds slowed down as if I was ready to reach out for the wolf to help him up to join us. We were high up in the tree making it difficult to really see him yet somehow everything around me faded and the wolf's face zoomed in to a point where I was gazing into his brown eyes from close enough to see the golden flakes in his irises.

Unnerved by the entire situation, everything in me screamed to move, hide, or jump from the tree as long as I hid the fact it was me who was controlling the air around us, but I couldn't move to save my life. I couldn't even speak to ask Char to do something. Anything at that point.

Much to my relief a shout came from somewhere in front of us, the loud bellow bouncing off the thick trunks. It repeated again a minute or so later while me and the wolf stood frozen in our stare off.

"Alaska!" Dimitri's voice came through that time loud and clear. "Charmaine!"

Loud snapping of branches and the rustling of leaves from where we were perched broke the connection I had with the wolf. My head whipped around thinking a vamp or a hyena managed to climb so they can attack us only to find Char emerging from the thick foliage holding a broken two finger thick branch in front of her like a sword.

I gaped at her like a fool, my jaw unhinging and dropping to my chest.

"We are here." She called out to the alpha and flicked her hair over her shoulder with the free hand. "Good thing you spoke so I can stop the winds. Last thing I want to do is hurt friends."

There was a leaf sticking out from one of her curls and for some dumb reason I found it fascinating. It was bobbing every time she turned her head and her hair bounced. It had my undivided attention for longer than it should've until my brain registered that she was waving the stick at the emerging shifters like a magic wand ready to spit spells at them.

Hysterical giggle bubbled up but I choked it down before it became audible.

The grey wolf growled from below us pebbling my skin with goosebumps, his ears pinned to the skull and his teeth bared. He was calling both of us liars there was no doubt there, so I ignored his existence. What else could I do? If it came down to it, it would be his word against ours and last time I checked it was one of him and two of us.

It all happened too fast.

"Look out!"

Dimitri's bellow was full of horror as it came at the same time with the vampire who sneaked up on us and threw himself at Char who was the bigger target standing up than me crouched down low enough my butt was touching the branch. The momentum turned both of them in a circle where Char's feet slipped off the branch and they plunged down toward the ground wrapped up like lovers around each other.

My friend's eyes were wide enough for me to see them clearly in the moonlight when we locked gazes, and the fear I saw in them took my breath away. There was desperation there too but also resignation which told me she expected me to do nothing. If she reached inside my chest and ripped my heart out with her bare hands it would've hurt less.

"Char!" Dimitri's shout turned into a roar at the end but I ignored him. There was nothing he could do because he was too far and they were already more than half way to the forest floor.

The vampire had his mouth open when I focused on him, the long sharp fangs aimed at my friend's jugular as he was preparing to strike like a viper. Char closed her eyes and an expression of serenity washed over her features. The wind was rustling her curls like wild springs around her face hiding most of the bloodsucker, but not hiding him enough that I couldn't see his mug. Rage exploded inside me so fast and so hot it blinded me for a split second and it slowed everything around me down to a crawl.

I saw Dimitri starting to shift, his shoulders bunching up and his face etched with a determination of a desperate man. Others were running behind him, Angela amongst them as well. I could appreciate his effort to protect me and save my friend but we both knew he wasn't going to make it on time.

The strangest thing was the grey wolf found this whole thing amusing and sat back on his hunches to watch it unfold. If I managed to save Char I was going to wax that wolf if it was the last thing I did. My ears were thundering so loud a migraine started pulsing behind my eyes.

"Do it. His life is yours to take." I could've sworn that Zin's voice whispered in my ear and reached me loud and clear through the noise deafening me. But that couldn't be since he was a figment of my imagination and lived in a weird dream.

Right?

Taking a breath and knowing full well this was the end of my life, I reached my hand toward Char who had her eyes open again and looked terrified. I didn't care who saw me do magic. The MPO could've stood under that tree for all I cared.

"*Thoir dhomh do bheatha.*" Give me your life, I commanded the vampire with my birthright, my outstretched fingers curled up into a fist so tight my nails sliced the skin of my palm. Warm liquid gathered inside my clenched fingers and trickled toward my wrist where it slid around it and fell toward the ground.

Everything was still moving in slow motion, each blink

of an eye lasting a full minute instead of a split second. Voices reached me but they were garbled like I was hearing them from underwater, so I ignored them, captivated by the rope of crystalline blue that snaked out from the vampire and attached itself to my fist.

It pulsed like a heartbeat and euphoria filled me when the lifeforce begam pumping into me. When I commanded his life to come to me he no longer found my friend tasty but his mouth stood open still. His mouth opened on a silent scream this time while his face grayed and shriveled as his whole body husked out before it hit the ground.

Char dropped next with a grunt.

She didn't move.

My eyes were still on my friend and I waited until I was certain her chest moved before I released the hold I had on time itself. Looking back, I should've been more careful, and used common sense if nothing else but in a situation when a loved one was in danger none of those things take precedence. You act first, think later.

At least I do.

The sound returned with a rush and that was when I heard the still warning shouts. Dimitri was now galloping on all fours toward the tree which told me he was running and shouting for me not my friend as I thought, his claws raking the forest floor hard enough to throw patches of dirt and grass behind him. Angela still in human form dropped on her knees next to Char but her gaze was fixed on me, the bright blue eyes glowing in the night full of shock.

I felt the hot breath first over my left shoulder rustling strands of my hair. My head started to turn so I could see who, and what, was behind me but internal sharp pain lacing through my torso forced me to fall forward with a scream so loud it shredded my vocal cords instantly. Almost as if whatever was inside me, dark and twisted used that opportunity to endcme once and for all.

Foolishly I thought for a moment that it was a perfect time for me to die that night. I revealed that I was a witch to save my friend. It was better to be killed instantly than taken in front of the MPO so they could prosecute and execute me publicly to make a point.

I could fight it I guessed, if I claimed I was a far-removed elemental through my family tree to explain the winds. There was no explaining draining the lifeforce of any living creature apart from witch magic, however.

Sharp teeth closed in on my neck and exerted pressure to a point of pain but didn't break skin. My body jerked out of survival instinct but went limp instantly after that. The darkness surrounded me and I welcomed death only to be denied it by none other than Dimitri Bell.

Damn him to hell.

"Stop! Let her go." Dimitri ordered with so much authority the rest of the wolves in the forest whimpered loudly while cowering behind anything they could find.

My eyes snapped open and shock like no other spread through me. Dimitri was talking alright, loud and clear as always, his accent thick and sending little zaps through my veins even in this situation. Death was still looming over me, the hot breath of the predator puffing over the side of my neck but he wouldn't bite to finish me off. There was only one problem with what I was seeing, too. In front of me there wasn't the man Dimitri that was standing who spoke with such authority. Oh, no. He was a wolf.

And he just spoke out loud.

In front of everyone.

Chapter Fifteen

The silence which followed turned the blood in my veins into ice. An oppressive feeling spread throughout the woods, laying down the blanket of expectation so thick you could cut it with a knife. My heart was doing its damn best to bust a hole in my ribcage so it could run and hide from the accusing eyes of everyone around us.

But I couldn't twitch a muscle.

I could barely breathe if I was being honest.

Held prisoner in the stormy gaze of Dimitri's wolf I stood still as a statue.

In the madness of the last moments of my life I yet again regretted that Char lost her memories of Damian to help me avoid prosecution. And she didn't even buy me a whole year of freedom for such a steep price. They must've had something very special for the Fates to take the Druid away from her as a counterbalance of the blood magic, I thought, not for the first time. I guess it bothered me more than I wanted to admit that she never disclosed that to me when I thought that we shared everything.

The vampire who had the misfortune of trying to kill me fell from the branch like a deadweight and the dull thump when he hit the ground made a cloud of leaves and debris arise.

He didn't move.

That made me drag my eyes away from the wolf and glance at my friend who was still on the forest floor, alive thank the stars, her head and the cloud of chestnut curls in Angela's lap. She was cradling one of her arms and there was blood caked in the hair stuck to her temple, but she was breathing. Warmth filled my numb body when we locked gazes and she offered me a faint smile as a tear trickled down her face. It was much easier to see when the shifters still on two legs moved the lights of their flashlights all over the place.

"What is the meaning of this?" A familiar voice snapped from somewhere to my right a second before Angela's father stepped into my line of sight.

My head turned to the side automatically when the flashlights illuminated his naked body and although my brain was overwhelmed with the information it was trying to process at the time one thing became abundantly clear. The old alpha came to that spot in the woods in his four-legged form. And since none of the others apart from Dimitri and Angela came anywhere near the tree Char and I used as a bastion, it was only fair to think he was the grey wolf.

With that realization I forgot all about the old man's nudity and looked at him. His face I mean, because I did my best not to allow my eyes to dip bellow his chest. Brown eyes the same as the grey wolf's narrowed down on me for a moment but they turned back toward Dimitri immediately full with fury.

I turned to Dimitri as well thinking I would find him worried or maybe cocky as usual ready to tell the world to step aside to let him pass. Instead, he watched me levelly, his stormy blue eyes scanning me from head to toe for injury and the relief there when he found nothing more than a few scratches was palpable. Anger spiked through my numbness at the audacity. How dare he worry about me when he all but screamed that he had witch blood too by talking in his animal form.

"Apprehend the witch." My head whipped around so I can glare at Angela's father who gave the order. "And don't try anything stupid or your friend will pay the price." The old man spat at me. "And you. Dimitri. What is the meaning of this?"

"He can't answer you right now." I heard my voice loud and clear and I realized I have spoken without meaning too.

Dimitri's eyes widened.

"Wait." The old alpha raised a hand and the handful of bulky males that were looking for a way up the tree where I was still perched froze. "Are you doing that to him, witch?"

Holding Dimitri's gaze for long enough that he knew he would owe me big time this time around, I jutted my chin out. "Of course, I am doing it. Which one of you useless creatures could do magic as refined as that if not me?"

"Release him from your spell." The old man stomped angrily over leaves and branches and pressed his foot into Char's neck. "Release him now!"

It would be a lie if I said I didn't debate for a split second to drain him and leave him as a husk but even I knew that would be a point of no return for me. At least so far, I had all minor offenses, petty theft and such. Maybe my soul would be able to find peace after they burn me for the world to see. Plus, I'd go happy knowing Dimitri Bell owed me for saving his ass.

Char gasped in pain when the soon to be dead alpha if he didn't step away from her put more pressure on her neck. The rage, which was always stewing and simmering, rushed toward the surface and I saw red.

"Remove your nasty talons from her face wolf or I'll turn your pretty daughter inside out. I'm pretty sure her tits will look better if the muscle and fat tissue is above skin. Don't you agree?"

"Allie, don't." Char rasped and clawed with her hand desperately trying to reach her tote. They removed it and placed it out of her reach when she fell.

"Oh, I will." I glared down at the old alpha. "I said remove your nasty tentacles from my friend or I will use your entire pack as poppets not just your soon to be son-in-law."

Wisely Dimitri stayed silent.

I had no idea what he was thinking talking like that.

"*Thig adhair, dèan mar a tha mi ag àithneadh.*" Come Air, do as I command. I swirled my hand and tossed the old man away from Char with a flick of a wrist because he wasn't moving fast enough. "I told you to move. Don't make me repeat myself."

"Release him." The old man pushed himself off the ground where I lobbed him and stood up. He was stubborn, I'd give him that much.

"I release you." I drawled to Dimitri who was gazing at me with calculation. I could almost hear his brain working behind the storms of his irises and it rubbed me wrong for some reason. Can he just be grateful we came a full circle and I was not as petty as I thought?

I saved his perky butt, a thank you would suffice.

I must've put a bit too much dramatics in my tone because in all the chaos Char snorted a laugh. She must've thought that I was being sassy, which wasn't necessarily untrue, but it was more than that. My secret was out one way or another. We could get away with it but we would have to kill most of Angela's pack and none of us, including myself, were going to do that.

Taking the blame and placing all the attention and a neon warning sign on me was the smartest thing to do.

The truth of Dimitri's bloodline would ruin his entire empire which his family had built for decades. It would be a great way to pay his father back for starting all this but I don't think the son deserved it. Plus, hopefully this meant he would look after Char and have her back if she ever needs it.

All train of thought screeched to a halt when Dimitri shifted back to his human form. Despite the situation my eyes scanned him from the top of his head to his toes and back. A vivid image of him standing next to me while we spoke to Zin came to mind but I brushed it away. This was neither the time nor place for interpreting dreams.

"Capture the witch." The old alpha sounded like a broken record. Also, it was hilarious that he was sending others to touch me but he stayed as far away from me as possible, "We will place her in the wine cellar and notify MPO to come and collect her."

"I will bring her to the cellar." Dimitri stabbed a leg in the sweats someone handed him. "They can check the parameter in case more of the vampires and hyenas are left roaming around."

A collective sigh could be heard as the members of the pack scurried left and right to do as Dimitri said. Not that it appeased the old man. I could tell he was gearing up for an argument as I decided to get down from the branch. On my own, thank you very much.

"We need to detain her and all of those creatures will be released from whatever spell she had them under." Angela's father snarled, staring daggers at me as I slipped and slid down the tree. "She must've used them so she could lure us here."

"For what reason would she lure us here father?" Angela spoke for the first time. She sounded tired.

"I don't want to find out." His hand sliced the air in agitation.

"So she spelled them to attack her and her friend, and they both almost died, just to bring us in the woods." Angela was like a dog with a bone, pun intended. "She could've just asked us to follow her if that was her intention."

"Don't be absurd, Angela, I would never follow a young woman to the woods." He looked at his daughter like she grew a second head.

"I would've." She told him simply. "If she wanted to kill me she had plenty of opportunities to do so. Her and her friend risked their lives to lure the spelled creatures away from the house so no one would get hurt."

"That's what she wants you to think." The old man grumbled but watched me differently through narrowed his gaze. "We need to hand her over to the MPO. They know how to deal with those like her."

"I am from MPO." Dimitri planted himself between me and the old alpha when my feet touched the ground. "I will take her to headquarters myself."

"She took control of you son. I know you feel the need to prove you are strong, I was your age once. But this one is not to be trusted. We need to sedate her so she can't use her powers."

"Because if I wanted, you would be quacking now and laying eggs, old man." I muttered under my breath but damn shifter hearing he heard every word of it.

My blood was buzzing under my skin. Some euphoria overtook my whole body the moment I took the blame for the magic and it thrummed through my veins like a melody. As if accepting out loud who and what I was made the universe celebrate my rebirth. It felt right claiming my birthright although I wished it was under different circumstances.

"You insolent whore." Angela's father spat at me, hatred burning hot in his gaze and twisting his features. Gone was the pleasant male who spoke to me at his party. "Don't you dare use your magic again, or I will make sure your death is drawn out."

"You won't be able to do anything if you are dead." I pointed out conversationally only to hear Char groan in exasperation. "What? I'm just saying. It's true."

"Tie her mouth with this so she can't speak." The old male shoved a necktie at Dimitri that one of his betas no doubt brought to him. The constant glazing of his eyes told me he was communicating with his pack while we discussed my death and the colorful names he was coming up with for me.

"I don't agree with that decision, Father." Angela rose from the ground and helped Char stand up, as well. "Something doesn't feel right about this."

"No one is asking you what you agree with. Last time I checked I was still the alpha of this pack." His voice was packed with alpha power and I watched the beautiful she wolf fight the compulsion to cower before him.

"Something feels off." Char leaned on me, allowing me to hold most of her weight up. "Help me get my tote, Allie. Shit is about to go down, I can feel it."

She was still talking when I slid toward the discarded purse and had to lift the handle with my foot like a monkey so I don't drop my bestie on the ground but I managed. Lucky for us Dimitri's shoulders were wide enough to hide us until we had Char's tote in our possession.

"That's the witch. The redhead." The old alpha said to someone I couldn't see from behind Dimitri.

"Who are they?" Angela straightened up and squarely faced her father. "What is going on?"

"Let them take the witch Angela and no one needs to get hurt. Step aside." Her father snarled, his tone full of impatience.

My head was spinning. What in the world was going on.

"I'm not moving an inch until you tell me what is going on. And she is not going anywhere." The blonde even flicked her high ponytail over her shoulder and cocked her hip. My respect for Angela grew tenfold no matter the reason she was defending me.

Why was she defending me?

"I am your alpha. Step aside." The old man barked at his daughter.

"Not anymore." Angela kicked off her sandals and planted her feet shoulder width apart. "I challenge you for your position in the pack."

"Oh shit." Char breathed sagging in my arms.

Chapter Sixteen

"What in the goddess name happened?" I muttered urgently while Dimitri dragged me to the side along with Char who was still clinging to me like a spider monkey.

"Angela challenged her father." He had the gall to mansplain things to little ol' me and I jabbed my elbow between his ribs in retaliation.

"I heard that, I'm not deaf. Why? Why did she do that? She doesn't even like me." My voice rose with each word, until I was practically shouting at him.

"Something is off with her father so she reacted. She has no chance of winning this fight." The grimness of Dimitri's tone sent a shiver down my spine. "She's not strong enough and I cannot get involved."

"We must do something." Char voiced what all three of us were thinking but we knew pack laws and we were not dumb enough to destroy what little chance Angela had by getting involved.

Just like us, many of the pack who were lingering around crept up closer to watch the standoff between a father and a daughter, forgetting all about the witch they wanted to destroy, for now. It worked for me as long as I get to keep breathing and no one threatened Char.

"I need the two of you to run." Dimitri tugged on my arm to get my attention faster. "Go! Take my car and drive out of LA as fast as you can. I will find you later." He shoved the key in my palm as if I was his trained puppy and I'd jump right on it.

I looked at him, unimpressed.

"Alaska, I need you to leave town until I can figure out a way to fix this." He told me on a sigh and Char was already shaking her head. "What? It's her life we are talking about here. This is not a game."

"If you say so." Char muttered, side-eyeing me like she expected me to foam up at the mouth and pounce on him like a rabid racoon.

"They will never stop hunting me now, Dimitri. That ship sailed the moment I threw caution to the wind and used my magic in public." After helping Char to stay up by leaning her on the closest tree I wiped my hands off my slacks out of habit. Surprisingly, I was not nervous at all.

"What do you think you are doing?" He hissed at me and tried to grab my arm to yank me back no doubt.

"I'm going to help your girl win." I sidestepped his attempt to hold me back. "If you think she's not strong enough to win against him and she challenged him because of me, then I'm going to even the odds."

"Allie, that is not our fight." Char chirped in with no conviction in her tone. "We should go, he has a point."

Angela and her father were still locked in their stand-off, their stares practically tangible as a heavy tension crackled between them like an electric current. I felt the intensity in their impasse almost viscerally - my skin erupting with goose bumps as all conversation around us hushed to nothing but hums in the background between the trees. Sensing the gravity of the situation and what that would mean for them, everyone seemed to choose a side. Interestingly enough, it seemed the daughter was better liked than the father. With me stepping toward Angela more and more wolves glanced at each other and saddled behind her back. Surprisingly they were led by the majority of the males from the pack. Who knew looking like a bombshell could help a girl win in pack politics?

A chill ran down my spine as I glanced sideways at Dimitri and saw his jaw tightened in determination.

Not so he could go help his wife-to-be, but to stop me from getting involved it seemed.

Selfishly, I needed him to knock it off so I could help Angela win this fight because the universe offered me a blessing that night. One I had no intention of ignoring. He couldn't be so self-centered that he wouldn't see the gravity of what was happening.

If the oath for the union of Dimitri and Angela was taken unwillingly by their fathers, then if one or both old alphas died the promise will be broken. In theory, since the power involved recognizes them as the root for the magic tying everything together, with death occurring everything should unravel.

It made sense to me as I said, theoretically.

In practice? We were about to find out.

I was ready to do everything to stack the odds in our favor.

Insanely enough for just a moment I thought maybe that's why Angela challenged her father. She wanted out of their engagement as much as I wished it didn't exist.

Which was dumb. Dimitri might be hot as hell but I didn't like him.

Yeah, I almost believed it too.

The pack either trusted Dimitri Bell too much and believed he could subdue a witch or they didn't believe the old alpha's accusations that I was one. None of them were paying close attention to us. Instead, they just gave us a passing glance or a raised eyebrow, which suited me just fine."

"Do you really want to go, Char?" Knowing my friend well enough I waited until she twisted her mouth in a grimace.

"No." Char huffed. "Just because he is right doesn't mean I want to listen. I was just saying. Playing, Captain Obvious if you will."

"I thought so." I felt better knowing my bestie was on the same page as me. "I think I got this. You stay here and just in case watch my back. From him, too." My forefinger stabbed the air in Dimitri's direction.

"I got you." She petted her tote, got comfy on the trunk that was holding her up and narrowed her eyes on Dimitri.

"You can argue or you can help." I told him making a split-second decision to point out what was at stake in case he missed it. "If she wins, the oath could be broken for your marriage. That's a best-case scenario if I'm not mistaken? If not, she wins, and you are now engaged to the alpha of the neighboring pack. I see that as a win-win."

"I can deal with the oath later. Your life is in jeopardy, Alaska. We need to get you out of here while they are preoccupied with the fight." He tried to reason with me, I'd give him that. Unfortunately, I was already committed to the idea of being Angela's fairy godmother.

"Can't they just start nipping at each other or something." Char was rubbing her arm, the one she was cradling to her chest. "Whatever it is that they are doing is making me want to claw my way out of my own skin."

"He is trying to force her to submit." Dimitri glared at Angela's father for the first time. "If he cam make her shift he's won half the battle."

"I don't think so." Ignoring the strange glances I received from a couple of the people closest to where we were standing, I shuffled to the side until I had a clear view of Angela but not so much her father.

My heart skipped a beat when I saw the female for the first time not looking like she was photoshopped into life. Her platinum hair which looked silver in the moonlight and the glow of the flashlights was plastered on the sides of her face. Her chest was heaving as she panted and her hands were clenched into fists at her sides. With obvious effort she was resisting whatever power her father was throwing at her to a point where her body was starting to tremble. I had to help her somehow while pretending I knew exactly what I was doing so Dimitri doesn't drag me out of the forest like the caveman he was.

How hard could it be to boost her power? If I could drain the life from someone I could do this, too. Right?

"*Neart an spioraid.*" Strength of spirit, I muttered curling my fingers like claws and turning my hand in a circle with obvious effort.

I figured if it's a mental war they were having, enhancing her spirit might work in our favor so I poured everything I had into it. It seemed like I overdid it a touch because Angela jerked in surprise and she stiffened her shoulders. Thankfully she didn't turn her head to look in my direction although she wanted to I could feel it. A connection formed between us like a rope attaching itself on both ends to our solar plexus.

"Is that all you've got?" She growled to her father, her usually sultry tone rougher and more animalistic.

"Stand down." Her father took a step forward, his shoulders bunching up as if he was preparing to pounce.

A shout lodged itself in my throat to warn her like that would've done much difference. The old alpha shifted so suddenly I kept blinking at the air where his upper body should've been longer than it was necessary. The grey wolf launched himself at Angela while she struggled with her own transformation. It's when I noticed that I was metaphysically gripping our connection for dear life and probably slowing her down, so following my instinct I simply let go of the control.

A whole new world opened for me that I didn't know existed. The moment Angela shifted into her wolf something strange and astounding happened. The woods, the people, the night…it all disappeared to reappear to me in the most astonishing way possible.

I was looking through the eyes of Angela's wolf.

Every movement was brought to my attention, including the rustling of the grass and leaves under her-mine? - paws. The wonder and elation of the new experience and sensation were lost when a sharp pain raked through the left side of my ribcage and my scream joined the howl of Angela's wolf. I wasn't just seeing through her eyes I was feeling everything she was feeling as well. The gravity of the situation pressed heavier on me when I felt warm liquid spread under my silky blouse.

"Alaska?" Dimitri's voice reached me but I couldn't see him at all. "What is happening?" he growled in my ear as he picked me up to his chest.

My body rocked with his movement and I realized he was running while holding me in his arms. Panic settled momentarily for Char and I prayed he didn't just leave her behind. Howls and snarls filled the night air and I watched transfixed as the grey wolf circled and tried to jump Angela's much smaller one from all sides. The bustard was going for the throat the majority of the time so I made sure not to ebb or stop the flow of magic channeling through me into the she wolf.

He raked his claws over Angela's spine and another scream was torn from me as I writhed and trembled in Dimitri's arms. Through all that pain and the thundering in my ears I could've sworn I heard Char yell something about me bleeding and her killing everyone. At least I knew she was doing good. He didn't leave her behind.

All thought stopped when a sudden surge of magic rushed through me as if Angela sucked it in with a gulp. Heat burst through our connection and the vision of her wolf turned hazy and red. I felt the intent before anything happened. The thirst for power, the triumph and lastly the regret before the teeth of Angela's wolf closed over her father's jugular. I even tasted the coppery taste of blood on my tongue before everything wavered and I lost consciousness.

The last thing I heard was the victory howl from Angela before I passed out.

The terrain shifted from grassy fields to rocky outcrops as I came to while we raced away from danger. The sounds of snarls and howls grew fainter as we moved further away, but were still close enough for unease to settle within me. I desperately hoped that I did indeed hear Char earlier and she wasn't back there with wolves who just lost their old alpha.

We eventually came to a stop in an open field encircled by trees where I could see stars twinkling above us like fairy lights even if they were spinning from the snap back reaction I got as I fully returned to my physical body. Dimitri carefully placed me down on my feet and I clung to him for support when my knees wobbled from the disorienting sensation. His face softened at the sound of my gasp and he seared me with his smoldering gaze in a way that made me feel like he hoped he could read my mind.

As fast as I could, I released my hold on him and stepped away.

Char moved closer to offer support and we held onto each other waiting and holding our breaths. Seconds that felt like hours crawled by until finally, after what seemed like an eternity, Angela emerged through the trees with only minor cuts and bruises visible on her naked body. She changed back into human form right after the kill and walked towards us with an air of confidence radiating off her as if nothing had happened at all. Her gaze was locked on me and there was no doubt that she knew what I had done. The bad part?

She didn't look impressed at all.

Maybe what I saw as an opportunity to set things straight was not a blessing at all.

But my energy was nearly depleted and black roses were blooming at the edges of my vision. I fought as much as I could but at the end exhaustion won and I succumbed to the darkness.

Chapter Seventeen

With a groan I rolled to my side in hopes not to vomit all over myself. Acid was burning the inside of my mouth and swallowing thickly I pushed the bile down. Why was my bed so hard and cold? With everything in me I prayed that I was not dead and this was not some sort of hell for me. Because let me tell you, nothing can be worse than an uncomfortable bed.

Faint sounds buzzed in the distance which were not cars driving by and that little thing had me snapping my eyes open. Owlishly blinking I rubbernecked left and right so I could get my bearings. A difficult task since only a faint light was flickering from somewhere far away giving me glimpses of shelving and if I was not mistaken a tall cabinet from medieval times. That almost made me laugh.

A large lump close to me moved and I squeaked as I practically bounced across the hard floor to get away from it. I was ready to lob it with whatever I could find if it attacked me until dark eyes locked on mine that I would recognize anywhere.

"Char?" I scrambled back toward her and yanked her into a hug. "Thank the stars you are okay." I squeezed her tight and stars burst behind my tightly closed eyelids. "Ouch!"

"Be careful, Allie." She peeled me off her and holding my arms to the side gave me a once over as much as she could've in the romantic set up they had going on for us.

"You should've led with that, Char. I know now to be careful without you telling me." I hoped my reassuring squeeze on her arm softened my sass. "Where are we? And tell me that you booked this hotel so I never let you forget it, please."

"In Angela's basement." Mouth twisted like she just tasted something sour, Char sagged where she was on the ground. "Dimitri argued we should be taken to a room or away from here but she gave him a long mute look, ordered us to the basement and him to follow her. That was over twenty four hours ago."

"How accommodating." My sarcasm was layered on thick. "Moderate temperature but the view sucks. One star, don't recommend."

"Can you get serious for one minute, please?" Jerking her tote in her lap she groused, giving me *the* look like an annoyed mother reprimanding her toddler. "We are held prisoners after you help that ungrateful, albeit beautiful, bitch win that fight. Which reminds me." her finger came up and pointed at the tip of my nose so I had to cross my eyes to see it. "Don't you ever do that to me Alaska McCullough! Do I make myself clear?"

"What am I not doing?" A thick fog had settled in my head so my brain was sluggish in sorting out information. I blinked innocently at her scolding face. "And before I forget I want to say I'm very proud of you for remembering to say something nice about Angela right after you called her an ungrateful bitch."

She grinned. "It's all about balance."

"Touché, my friend." With another groan I pressed a hand to my belly hoping it'll keep the bile back and wiggled closer to her. "More importantly, please tell me you have something in that bottomless pit of a bag that can get us out of here."

"Unfortunately, nothing works. I've been trying anything I could think of." Her foot did little circles as if she was loosening the muscles of her ankle. "I even kicked the door at one point." Turning the same foot to the side, she showed me the dark bruise smudged over her skin. "For all the good it did. I think they have some talismans on the other side that are counteracting my potions."

If looks could burn doors she would've eviscerated the one we were eyeing from across the space which was keeping us locked up.

"Okay." With a fortifying sigh I pushed myself off the ground.

"What are you doing?" Char gasped and grabbed my hand so she could pull me back down. "You were dead for close to a day, Allie. You need to rest first."

"I'm just going to try and open it." My jutting chin pointed at the door. "What are the odds that they have talismans against witch magic?" Cocking my head I rocked it left and right as if debating the said odds. "My guess is none."

"I don't know what you did to help Angela win, but it took everything from you. I honestly thought you were dead. Even your pulse was barely there, Allie." Tears glistened in my friend's eyes and a fist squeezed my chest. "We can wait a bit longer and try later maybe? You should rest more."

"I feel okay, I promise." Crouching so we can be level eyed I took her hand in mine. "Let me try open it and I will tell you everything. I doubt anything will stop me but who knows."

Char nodded since she couldn't talk by the looks of it, Her lips were pressed in a thin line whitening at the edges. I wanted to slap Angela for stressing my friend out like that. She really was an ungrateful bitch.

"You can ask, you know." Char mumbled conversationally and when I looked back at her over my shoulder she pretended to straighten out the permanent wrinkles on her dress.

"Ask what?" Facing the door I pressed my hand on it and closed my eyes. "I can see that you are banged up but okay. I can totally live with that. After running through a forest hanging off of trees like monkeys, and fighting crazed vampires and hyenas it is to be expected to be battered and bruised. No?"

"I think it worked." She said barely above whisper.

Whatever spells they had on the door were vibrating under my palm strong enough to warm up my skin. Like cats they rubbed on my power seeking attention, or luring me into false safety was more like it. I focused on the power trying to latch onto it and destroy it that way but it kept slipping away and being elusive. After the few times I kept at it I shoved away from the door in frustration.

"I think I'm going to go through it." I told Char not turning around to look at her. "What worked?"

I took a deep breath and got ready to speak the spell. "*À se...*"

"The oath that was binding Dimitri and Angela broke."

My friend's tone was soft almost tentative but I heard it so loud the spell I was going to cast lodged in my throat and choked me. "She didn't sound thrilled about it, in case you were curious."

"I didn't think she would be." Clearing my throat, I was too afraid now to face Char in case I find judgment in her eyes. Not that I'd blame her for it. I was a horrible person for wishing to free him from his commitments, willingly accepted or not. "Was he thrilled to be free?"

I had to ask.

"I don't know, Allie." Char sucked in a deep breath before releasing it slowly. "He was livid when he stormed out of here, I didn't get a chance to ask. She accused him of planning all of it, though."

"Lovely." Scrubbing a hand over my face I pressed the bridge of my nose to relieve the headache building there. "I'll deal with it later and only if I must. Stay here, I'll be right back."

"Really, I just wanted to take a stroll first." Char drawled and I couldn't help the snort.

"I won't be long." Shaking off my hands to rid myself of the nerves, I blew out air strong enough to rustle my matted hair. "*À sealladh.*" Out of sight, I commanded and didn't need a mirror to know that it worked when magic buzzed through my entire body.

Touching the door again I applied pressure and ordered it to Open. "*Fosgailte.*" Well aware that Char was silently watching me from behind. "I remembered everything from the night when I connected to my mother's journal, too. I'll tell you all about it when I get back. Let me find us a way out of here."

"Thank you." She told me primly. "This dusty ground is not suitable for a goddess like me."

"I agree." Snickering I stepped forward to pass through the door and promptly smacked my nose and forehead into solid wood hard enough to make my eyes water. "What in the stars?"

"What happened?" Char jumped to her feet. "You'll need to make yourself visible because I have no idea how to help if I can't see you."

"You are still here, aren't you?" She asked after a short pause while I kept cupping my nose and hoping I don't end up bruised like a panda.

"Yeah." My muffled reply had her frowning. "It didn't work, I can't pass through."

The shock of my magic not working more than anything else had me releasing the spell and becoming visible. We stared at each other, Char and I, silently for a long moment, understanding the implications of that for us.

"Why do they have protections against witch magic?" A heavy feeling of trepidation dropped like a rock in my stomach. "A better question, yet, why wasn't Angela's father surprised he had a witch on his running grounds?"

"I don't know and right now I don't even care." Char's foot started tapping. "What I do know however, is that, the moment that door opens I'm going to melt the skin off the person's face and we are skedaddling out of here."

"I love the way you think, your Divine Holiness." My attempt at bowing was poorly executed but she nodded regally nonetheless.

"Thank you, peasant, you can prostrate yourself at my feet when we get out of here." Tossing curls over her shoulder she shuffled left and right until she found herself a perfect position. "It's been almost a day, someone should be checking on us shortly."

"I hope so." The words were not yet out of my mouth

when both our heads jerked to our left where the scraping sound could be heard. "Please tell me you hear that." I whispered.

Char nodded vehemently, her corkscrews bouncing wildly around her face.

The sound came louder and stronger after a few heartbeats and we both scurried away from it toward the opposite side of the room. Something scraped over the stone or brick and it set me on edge. Not willing to chance it and let whatever or whoever it was to harm Char first I pushed her behind me although I was the shorter of the two of us. Her muttering in Italian told me she didn't appreciate it but tough luck for her.

I had a timer ticking on my life, she didn't. I was planning on keeping it that way. So, when she attempted to elbow her way out and stand next to me I grabbed her forearm and turned her invisible.

"À sealladh." I finished with a growl because she pinched me as hard as she could. "Thank you would've worked too." I hissed at her.

More scraping could be heard from the other side of the room and I fully expected a sea of rats to burst out of the wall and rush us. A shiver passed through me at the thought which made Char chuckle like some swamp hag. She probably though her pinch had me shivering in my pumps which by some miracle survived everything, fight and all.

We both squealed when tentacles burst from the wall, wiggling at us like some octopus on steroids. My brain was struggling through the fog muddling through it to understand what I was seeing but Char had no problem reacting. Her arm was in her tote one second and the next a glass bottle full of yellow liquid went sailing in the air.

It hit the wall with a crash and the tinkling of broken

glass before exploding into a ball of fire. The angry octopus didn't make a sound but it did wiggle its tentacles faster. What neither of us expected was the familiar voice of a man that started spitting explicatives colorful enough to ensure my face matched my hair. More thick cords burst through the wall making the house groan and I ducked instinctively as if that would save me if the roof collapsed over our heads.

"Why is it still alive?" Char shrieked in frustration clawing at my shoulder as she twisted this way and that looking up and probably expecting us to be buried alive.

"Why are you asking me? Last time I checked there was no octopus living on solid ground."

"That's a nice way to greet the person who's trying to save you." A man emerged from all the writhing tentacles and although he was covered in dust thanks to Char's nifty trick, I recognized him immediately. It's at the same time I saw what was breaking the wall and it wasn't an octopus. Roots were digging through brick and mortar breaking a path for him to pass.

"Damian!" My excited shout was met with a groan that whipped the grin off his face.

I looked at Char in shock.

"It's the Druid." She made a face like she would rather be a prisoner than be saved by him.

A shrug was her answer to my raised eyebrow.

Chapter Eighteen

"Thank you for coming for us." I told the Druid while we pushed our way through the tunnel the roots had made. "I couldn't pass through the talismans they placed on the door and walls. For whatever reason they work against my magic."

"They don't have talismans protecting anything." Damian said cryptically without turning to look at us.

"What do you mean?" speeding up my footsteps I hurried to keep up with him. My legs were much shorter so I had to work double time to keep up with the Druid.

Char was dragging her feet and pouting for some reason.

"It's all witch magic." Not even the steady nonjudgmental tone of his voice could've softened the blow.

"What?" I didn't mean to shout so loud but I couldn't care less who heard me.

"I don't know what is going on here, Alaska, but that much I can guarantee you. Witch magic is set on the parameter of the grounds. Its as thick as a fog as soon as you enter pack lands." He turned to look at me over his shoulder, the runes pulsing gently on his skin in the darkness. "I'm surprised you didn't feel it."

"I was too nervous to feel any...Wait a minute. Is the protection set to make you feel like you want to turn around and leave?"

"Yes, quite a strong compulsion."

"I felt it." I cursed under my breath for my stupidity. I should've known something was off. "They were waiting on us. The protection, the flowers placed on the fountain, the zombified vamps and shifters...all of it."

"It would appear so." He said softly not pausing in his even gait.

"Was the challenging of the alpha also planned?" Char made me jump when she spoke from next to me.

So, focused on what the Druid was telling me I didn't hear her join us. I was grateful she did because I laced my arm through hers or I would've sat down. The gravity of the set up punched me square in the chest. How could we be so blind. We played straight into their hands.

"No, it was not." Damian didn't look back that time, his long legs eating up the ground.

"We need to go get Dimitri, too." I rushed to tell him in case his escape route was taking us away from the mansion. "He is stuck arguing with Angela since she broke the oath when she killed her father."

"She wouldn't have killed him on her own, She had help. Didn't she?" Again his tone held no accusation or judgment.

So, I shrugged although he couldn't see me. "She did have help. And for the record I don't regret it." After thinking about it a second I amended the statement. "I didn't regret it until she thought she was too tough and locked us in the basement. I would like to give her a piece of my mind now though."

"I bet you do." Damian chuckled good-naturedly but there was something off about the moment and it was bothering me enough to ensure the feeling wouldn't go away.

I gripped Char's arm tighter. "Hey, how did you figure out where we were?" My friend stiffened next to me but I ignored it. "I don't remember Char or Dimitri mentioning they called you before we joined the party."

"I've felt your magic once, Alaska. I can sense it anywhere now." He was walking fast so we were basically jogging to keep up with him.

"Oh, okay." I huffed, playing dumb but my mind was going avhundred miles an hour. "How convenient. You're basically a personalized Alaska tracking device, huh?" My giggle was forced, strained and high-pitched.

"You could say that." His low laugh sounded almost ominous firing up alarms in my head.

"Anyway, I'm really glad you could track us here." The low light of dawn peaked in the distance and my heart jumped in my chest. "I want nothing more than to get out of here and put all of this behind us."

Char was searching for something in her tote, her frown telling me she couldn't find it. We were running out of time now that the exit of the tunnel was getting closer and if she had no potion that she could use it was up to me to keep us safe. Not because I didn't trust Damian. Quite the opposite actually. After everything that happened to me the last few days I was finding it difficult to believe just my eyes.

I'd doubt I was looking at Char if my intuition told me something was off.

The hyenas and vampires, pure example of it.

"We are almost there."

Char nudged me with her arm to show me she had a talisman in her hand. I blinked at it not understanding and she jabbed it in my palm losing patience with me. In her other hand she had one of her potions gripped tightly between her fingers ready to pitch it at the back of Damian's head. It felt wrong to allow her to attack him so I reached over and snatched it from her.

If the Druid was going to feel betrayed I rather he aimed that at me not Char.

I cost the two of them too much already.

"Whatever you are planning, I suggest you wait until we exit the tunnel, Miss McCullough." Damian said, almost cordially.

My arm was already cocked back so I could toss the potion at him but Char grabbed my forearm to stop me. She didn't say anything only shook her head barely perceptively and since I've never known my best friend to be overly cautious I froze immediately. My throat tightened with such strong emotions I almost choked on it.

How hard must it be for Char to be willing to fight Damian?

Not that she remembers what she felt for him but I've seen her steal glances occasionally. It's still there. Their connection. I know it as well as I know my own name.

I lowered my hand and jerked my head once in a nod to tell Char I wouldn't do anything to the Druid. She was still frowning and watching his retreating back as if it had all the secrets of the universe.

"Please don't act impulsively, and hear them out before you decide what you want to do." This time Damian turned to glance at us over his shoulder and with that cryptic comment stepped out of the tunnel.

"I actually want to turn around and go sit back in that

basement after that comment." I screeched to a halt and yanked Char back with me.

"If they have a seer, they already know what we would do." My bestie mumbled distractedly while searching her bag.

"We don't even know if it's the witches waiting for us out there." Gnawing on the inside of my mouth I watched her turn her purse this way and that. "Does this mean they have Angela and Dimitri? And why is Damian so nonchalant about it?"

"Here, put this on." Char pulled a necklace over my head, the talisman dangling heavy on it. "It won't stop an assault of magic but it'll hold it off long enough for you to find cover."

"And you?" I was already pulling my head out of it when she stopped me.

"I have one, too." She showed me the same one in her other hand.

"I'm really not in the mood for this shit." My grumbling had my bestie snickering. "I'd like to be put on time out for like a month. I'll reconsider joining the shit show after that."

"Wouldn't it be nice?" She said dreamily and despite myself I laughed.

Chances are we were getting captured or killed.

"Ready?" I took a deep breath before taking her hand.

"As ready as I'll ever be." With a reassuring squeeze she squared her shoulders and lead us out of the tunnel.

We were both a mess with matted hairs and sticks and leaves sticking out everywhere but the sorceress looked every bit the goddess she claimed herself to be. I on the other hand shuffled behind her slouching and hating life. My whole body hurt and I was sick and tired of everything.

What I needed was a week-long sleep, a spa day and

about seventeen cups of coffee. Why seventeen you'd ask? Because why the hell not? I could die at any moment; might as well enjoy what time I had left.

Char stepped out into the darkening evening. I mistook the light from afar as the sun coming up, but it seemed it was going down. Quite appropriate for the situation. What waited for us outside on the other hand was not.

Women stood in a semi-circle facing the opening in the ground from which we emerged. In all stages of life, they all had one thing in common, their long hairs nearly touching the small of their backs. One of the reasons I kept my hair above my shoulders in length. Witches saw their tresses as extensions of themselves and no witch worth her magic would allow scissors anywhere near her hair.

There was so many of them it was overwhelming and I had to fight my instinct to run. That's why when Char stopped to face them and snapped her back straight like a soldier I wobbled on my pumps next to her and gazed tiredly at the bunch. Not surprisingly, the same woman that was in our shop looking for a candle before the hyenas showed up, stood at the front of them.

"The Dreamcatcher." The whisper spread like a cloud of buzzing bees over the group and they all watched us with wide eyes, some of then leaning to whisper things to the person next to them.

Damian was to the side, his face expressionless and his body at ease. It should've told us there was no danger, since he was a friend but what my eyes were seeing said otherwise.

"Miss McCullough." The lady stepped forward. "We would like you to come with us."

Rubbernecking around told me the mansion was at our back far enough for them to have time to escape if the wolves decided to attack but not far enough for me not to see the outlines of the people watching through the windows.

"Listen lady, it's been a rough month or so and I have blisters on my feet from these dumb pumps. If I knew, which I should have now that I think about it, I would've come to the party wearing flipflops. So, go ahead and try to kill me because I'm not going anywhere with you or anyone else. I'm tired."

"Kill you?" She gasped like I just offended her mother or something. Even her hand pressed to her chest like she couldn't believe what she was hearing.

Collective gasps and muttering spread around the rest of them, as well.

Rage bubbled up inside me.

"Seriously?" I had to forcefully hold myself back so I don't walk up to her and punch her in the nose. "You destroyed my business, my home and my life. What else would you call it?"

"We've been trying to protect you, Alaska." A line etched itself between her brows showing she was actually much older than she looked. "The moment your existence was discovered we got involved. It was hard to reach you and warn you when they were everywhere." That last bit was spat out with venom. "If the situation was not dire we never would've come out of the shadows and brought attention to our coven."

"What in the stars are you talking about?" Dread was pooling in my stomach with each word spoken. Somewhere deep down I knew what was coming and I hated it more than I've hated anything else in my life.

Char grabbed my hand and squeezed so tight she cut off the circulation to my fingers. She was adding two and two as well by the looks of it. The woman's face softened when she undoubtedly saw the desperation in my eyes.

"You look so much like your mother." She breathed with tears in her eyes and I flinched like she slapped me. "I will explain everything but I need you to come with us. You and your friend, before the pack manages to push through our wards. We can only hold them back so long."

"And I should trust you why?" My resolve to run was disolving like a sugar cube in a glass of water.

"The wolves want to have you under their thumb so they can keep you ignorant of who and what you are. If you are not properly trained they can and will use you as a tool. We should've had this conversation long before now if Anastasia did what she promised. Dimitri Bell, her son, was sent to LA to find you and bring you to us. He failed."

Betrayal is a bitter pill to swallow, I'd say that much.

It burned fast and hot in my chest. I'd never felt so stupid.

I should've known.

"And we are sure that you're not lying how?" Char spoke for the first time her hold on my hand as tight as ever.

"You don't need to trust me. You can trust her because she will show you." The lady pointed with her hand at a woman walking toward us. "This is our seer."

Long white hair fell loose over her shoulders and it reached the back of her knees. I would've thought she was blind but her eyes were keenly locked on something to my side. When I glanced I realized it was Damian she was looking at and the Druid returned the attention with a soft fond smile I'd never seen on his face.

"Damian." The seer grinned back when she reached us.

"Mother." The Druid bowed his head and the ground shifted under my feet.

Char holding my hand was the only thing holding me up.

I felt numb.

"Would you come with us, please?" The lady gazed at me hopefully.

"We will come." Char answered because I couldn't. my tongue was too thick for my mouth. "Whatever it is we will hear you out before we decide what to do. And you stay away from us traitor." She snapped at the Druid when he took a step to join us.

"Thank you." The lady didn't wait a second longer in case we changed our minds. "Let's go."

They all moved as one, excitement adding pep to their steps. I let Char lead me wherever she wanted but I turned around to look at the mansion over my shoulder. Dimitri lied about everything hoping to use me as a power tool. How typical of him. If what the witches were saying was true indeed, I had every intention on destroying Dimitri Bell.

Hopefully he could see my glare from that damn house, too.

"We will hear them out then go, Allie." Char was mumbling close to my ear. "We can fight our way out if we need to. How bad can it be?"

I squeezed her hand in answer because I was too overwhelmed to talk.

How bad can it be, indeed.

We were screwed.

More by Maya Daniels

vinci-books.com/restingwitch

I didn't mean to unleash hell. But here we are.

I was the dud of my coven—until a failed spell blew up the library and unlocked my magic. In my panic, I tried a simple spell, but instead, I destroyed ancient texts, wrecked half the building, and somehow ended up half-naked in the high priest's office. Now, I'm totally screwed.

Turn the page for a free preview…

Resting Witch Face: Chapter One

Lesson 1: *don't drink and drive.*

No, scratch that. That was for humans. The real lesson was: don't drink and pretend you're something you are not. Like, acting like a badass witch when you have zero magic. Take it from me because it'll destroy your life. Although that was neither here nor there, when it came to me, since I was screwed the day I popped out of my mother's vagina. She died during childbirth, most probably out of disappointment. I kid you not.

I was a dud born in the most powerful bloodline of witches in the world.

How was that for a sap story?

"Hey, buddy," I called out like we're the best of friends. "Get back down here before you hurt yourself and I get blamed for it. What do you say?" The Kishi demon cocked his head and eyed me like I'd lost my mind. Poor schmuck had no idea that ship had sailed years ago.

My foot wobbled in my designer ankle boots when I

took a step forward, and I did an awkward shimmy-wiggle-swan-dive before I regained my balance. It was what happened when you drank one too many Manhattans and answered a call from your coven to deal with a demon selling illegal merchandise.

"Damn you! If I scratch my boots I'm going to skin you alive just to make myself a new pair. I should've just stayed in the damn bar." The racket of a paint can crashing to the floor and rattling around applauded my muttering. It also stabbed my brain, which was pounding like a shifter in heat when a willing body accidentally stumbled in front of his dick. Don't ask me how I know this, because as brutally honest as I am, I'm not going to tell you.

iPhone held in front of me the same way those pompous asses from the Magi Police waved their badges around, I pointed the flashlight right into the creep's eyes. It screeched like a banshee and scattered further into the darkness while I hissed curses at it. Luckily for the demon, none of them would be taking root, because ... no magic, duh.

What took my coven mates so long to get to the warehouse? If this was a party they'd be lining up at the door since yesterday. As I looked around the dirty warehouse and the misty odor of congealed blood and decaying bodies made my stomach roll, I couldn't say I blamed them.

The fact that Kishi demons had an attractive human face on the front and a hyena's face on the back of their skull was the least of my problems. Kishi demons used their human face as well as their smooth, luring voice and other tricks to attract unassuming idiots— which I definitely was not, shut it I'm not!—and then they proceeded to eat them with their deformed jaws. That would've been fine and dandy if they kept it under wraps, but this one also made an entire collection of body parts to sell on the magical black market. Quite a smart trick when the market was scarce, but not such a great idea for this guy, because he was dumb enough to get caught. That was *if* I managed to hold him back until the others got to the warehouse. With all the alcohol in my blood system, I got this like a hot potato in a bare hand.

Witches more than other supernaturals paid good money for body parts like the ones stacked all the way to the ceiling in the large building, although nobody liked to talk about it. It was that pink elephant in the room we all ignored. No delusions clouded my mind that my coven would "confiscate" the evidence in the warehouse without blinking an eye. I was basically standing in the middle of a gold mine.

The pentagram tattoo on the side of my forefinger tingled, an annoying reminder when my body thought I should be using magic, as adrenaline raced through my veins. My meat suit never got the memo we were shooting blanks. We were as impotent as Mike, my coven's administrator, according to Sissily.

"Go away witch, or die," the demon cooed, his alluring voice gliding over my skin like a caress and leaving goosebumps in its wake.

"Aww, you actually think I'm a witch." My eyelashes fluttered in his general direction as I stumbled deeper into the warehouse. "How adorable," I deadpanned, a serious expression on my face that froze him in his tracks.

Silence followed.

"Ah, you are the useless one." His face poked through the shadows before he fully emerged to sneer at me from over ten feet up, crouched like a gargoyle on the rafters. "I've heard of you. Pathetic." He dismissed me, as his full lip curled over a row of flat, white teeth.

Stolen Oath

I hated sneering. It reminded me too much of the looks on my coven mates every time they stared in my direction.

Shaking my head to regain my focus, I swallowed hard when the alcohol tried to come up. All I had to do was keep the hellspawn from escaping until reinforcements arrived, but he was pushing his luck. Even a dud could do that if said dud was not a little drunk and teetering on six-inch heels. I eyed my precious boots for a split second, considering using them as a weapon and chucking them at his head, but I changed my mind. Like hell I would mess up a good pair of designer boots for a stupid demon.

The choice was taken from me when he decided to try a trick called monkey in a circus and sailed through the air, aiming his body straight at me. My phone jerked to follow the arch of the jump, and I had one second of an "oh shit" moment before our bodies collided. Never mind me, my iPhone flew from my fingers, crashed on the concrete floor with a resounding crack, and I heard my silk shirt rip at the shoulder when we tumbled on the dirty concrete floor. I just bought that phone.

I saw red.

Fingers hooked like claws, I went straight for his eyes when he tried to straddle me. Somewhere in the back of my mind I was aware that if he bit me the poison from his kind would kill me in less than an hour, but I had liquid courage, louder than the alarm bells cheering me on. The demon didn't expect me to claw at his eyes, so when my nails made squelching mush out of his eyeballs, his human face roared at me. If I was in the right mind, I would be shaking in my skin. As things were, he resembled a chihuahua nipping at my ankles to my muddled brain. Wretchedly vile breath melted my makeup and I gagged, barely holding back the bile so I didn't puke all over both of us.

"It's called a toothbrush, asshole." I hacked hard enough to cough out a lung while jamming my forearm in his throat to hold back his snapping jaws. The Kishi demon was trying to munch on my face, for fuck's sake. "You should use it, damn you."

Desperate times called for desperate measures, and, as much as it pained me, I had to sacrifice my boots. My leg swung up like a slingshot, caught him on the side of the head, and he went down hard. His head bounced off the concrete, and his skull cracked with enough strength to be heard over the heartbeat in my ears. The air whooshing out of him satisfied my need to hurt him like he hurt my poor blouse. It was also new and cost me an arm and a leg. Using the time I had, I scrambled on my knees, yanked my poor boot off, and nailed him in the neck with the heel. The demon gasped, probably still dazed from the kick, but apart from a few spastic jerks, he didn't attempt to flee. Or move again at all, but that would be semantics.

They might think that was how I found him.

Right.

With a sigh, I dropped on my haunches not a moment too soon before the solid thump of feet came from the entrance behind me. Light jiggled up and down over the stacked shelving from the flashlight the person held, and I looked down my shoulder at the flipping piece of silk that used to be a soft olive color. Dirt, sweat, and dried blood from the scrapes on my upper arm turned the silk some disgusting color of brown. I frowned at the flapping fabric.

"Hands up where I can see them," the owner of the flashlight barked from behind me.

Great. Instead of my coven mates, I had to deal with a human cop. Just my luck for the night, it seemed.

"Do I look dangerous to you?" My head twisted so I

could squint at him over my shoulder, and a bright light stabbed me in the brain like a pickaxe. "Are you trying to blind me on purpose, or is this how you pick up chicks all the time? If they have a flashlight burning their retinas they can't see your ugly face, huh?" Oh yeah, I recognized the voice better than I should've.

"Hazel? What in God's name are you doing here?"

"Getting a tan. You?" I chirped brightly and regretted it when acid filled my mouth. I would never drink again.

"Don't be a smartass. I'm seriously asking what—" His words stopped when he noticed my ripped shirt and one bare foot, and he shuffled closer. I was pretty sure having my skirt bunched up around my hips and flashing the creases of my ass didn't help, either. Goddess, I looked a mess.

"Are you hurt?" His hulking frame kept moving closer, sending my heart to gallop in my chest.

"No, wait." My sudden shout stopped him in his tracks. "Stay there, Davon, you don't want to get bitten." Think Hazel, think.

"Bitten? What the hell, Hazel. Get away from there right now. What's in there?" When a gun cocked, I knew the jig was up. If he saw the demon, there was no doubt in my mind I'd be in more trouble than I already was.

"It's a dog, okay. Stay back because if you spook it, it'll bite me. Then I'll be pissed. Do you want that?" Where the hell was my coven?

"What kind of a dog?" Tone dripping with suspicion, his feet scraped the floor as he cautiously moved closer again. If he saw the Kishi starfishing it, not even my grandmother could cover the mess up.

"You are the one with a flashlight, Davon, so why don't you tell me. I'm not playing games when I tell you to stay back. Look at my face." I added an additional scowl for good measure, shuffling on my knees to hide the Kishi sprawled a couple of feet away, deep enough in the shadows not to be visible for the moment.

"What about it?" I could've laughed at the weariness in that loaded question, but he did stop coming closer.

"Does it say approachable to you right now?"

"It never does," he muttered, and I grinned at him like a fiend. "This is crazy. You don't get to boss me around after you dumped me."

"I already parted with my right boot, and I love these boots. You wanna try the left one? I can nail you in the forehead or in the jingleberries. Your choice," I threatened while internally freaking out. Being a bitch to Davon wouldn't work much longer. It never did. He would do the opposite of what I told him just to spite me. I could feel it.

"Hello," a female voice called from the entrance of the warehouse, and I deflated like a balloon recognizing my best friend Sissily. About freaking time. The demon was dazed, but he wouldn't stay down much longer. And if he woke up with Davon here, I had a nagging feeling my body parts would join those scattered around the warehouse in jars. Courtesy of my grandmother, of course. The demon didn't have shit on her when that witch got pissed.

"Stop right there. Police." Davon pointed his gun and flashlight at Sissily's face. Protecting her poor eyesight with a forearm flung in front of her, she blinked at him as if ready to say something.

"Is this your dog?" I rushed to say before she screwed me over. You never knew what would come out of her mouth. "It might be injured, it almost bit me."

"Hazel …" Davon started in a warning tone.

"Yeah, oh thank goodness you found him," Sissily

gushed, overdoing it a little, if you asked me. Whatever Davon wanted to say was silenced, thank the goddess.

"If this is your dog, Ma'am, I must report it, I'm afraid. It attacked a civilian, and it's considered dangerous." Davon, the good cop he always was, started reading Sissily her rights while she rolled her eyes.

I sighed, pinching the bridge of my nose.

"Oh, shut up human." Her hand flicked when she had enough of his word vomit, and she zapped him hard enough the poor guy convulsed a long moment before he passed out, the gun and flashlight clattering on the concrete.

Then she turned her blue peepers my way and gave me a once-over. Although her blonde hair was smooth and all in one place, and her pencil suit was sharp enough to cut a finger off, Sissily had no right to grimace at me. Someone should tell her "I bit a rotten lemon" was never a good look on a chick. Just saying.

"If you say a word Im'ma boob punch you." Pushing off the ground, I swayed, and for the second time I failed to glue the ripped silk sleeve together. "Are you alone?" It was improbable, but a girl could hope.

"The others are not far behind me. I had a feeling you'd jump right into this, so I made sure I came before anyone else. What do we have?" She sashayed closer, giving Davon a disgusted look.

"Kishi demon." I glared at the asshole who finally stirred with a groan.

"How do you find yourself in these situations, Hazel?" Ignoring her, I was still messing with the sleeve, so with a sigh, she took her jacket off and handed it to me.

"Thanks." Limping a couple of steps forward, I plucked it from her fingers. "And I wasn't kidding about the boob punch. I'll even twist your nipple until you scream if you don't keep your voice down."

"You do know we're not five anymore, right?"

"What's your point?"

I could tell she had so much to say just by the tightening of the tendons on her neck. Her throat worked, her mouth opening and closing until she gave up and shook her head.

Yeah, exactly my sentiments.

"Where's your other boot?" She followed the elaborate swirl of my finger until it pointed at the demon. My beautiful, precious boot was sticking out of his throat, covered in black blood and gore. Then she arched an eyebrow, which should've looked stupid on anyone except me, but on Sissily everything looked good. If she wasn't my best friend and if I had magic, I would've hexed her with warts. I hoped the girl knew how lucky she was that I loved her like a sister. What surprised me more was she loved me back the same, even though I was an asshole. At least most of the time.

"I've always told you fashion is a weapon if you learn how to use it. Did you believe me? Of course you didn't." My smirk earned me a twitch of her mouth. If anyone knew Sissily they'd know it for the huge win that was. She never smiled on a job.

"Danika is going to lose her shit." We both shivered at that.

As if saying the name conjured her, my grandmother's power preceded her presence, filling the warehouse with magic and saturating the air with the strong scent of ozone.

"Hazel Byrne." I flinched when my name echoed in the silent building, and Sissily copied me sympathetically. "Show your face this instant." My grandmother swooped in like a hungry vulture honing-in on a roadkill.

Me. I was the roadkill.

Thankfully, the lights came on inside the building, blinding me momentarily as thumps of many feet scattered throughout the warehouse. Our coven mates spread around the vast space like ants. I blinked like an idiot a few times until my vision cleared, and that was when I saw the look on her face. Cold, emerald eyes sharp enough to cut a diamond rolled over me from head to toe, assessing and judging while telling me she found me lacking in many ways. I gulped and tugged Sissily's jacket closer. Then Danika's unreadable gaze fell on Davon, who took a lesson from the Kishi demon and was starfishing it in the middle of the damn place. She stilled at the sight of a human cop and stabbed me with a glare afterwards.

"That was Sissily, not me." The words burst from me so fast I almost spit on my lower lip.

"Snitch," my best friend hissed, but her chin jutted out and she stepped closer to me.

"Every bitch for herself, remember?" I mumbled behind my hand when I raised it to wipe my mouth in case I was still drooling. Those Manhattans were buzzing in my head like a cloud of bees and making my tongue too thick for my mouth while I swayed where I stood. Oh boy was I screwed.

Sissily snorted but coughed to cover it up. Her reaction earned me a disapproving look from my grandmother, which I felt all the way to my soul. The woman saw everything no matter how hard I tried to hide it, and her hearing was better than a vampire's. I didn't have to guess because I *knew* she heard us.

I was the best fighter they had in our coven. Hand-to-hand or weapon combat, I could take them all down, and that included our high priest. But thanks to my lack of magic, I somehow always ended up looked down on, especially by Danika Byrne. Even when I did get the job done.

One demon stabbed in the throat with a designer boot, case and point.

"We will speak back at the coven." With flare, she spun on her heel, her long dress billowing behind her as she stormed out of the warehouse and left me grinding my teeth.

"Let's go." Linking her hand through mine, Sissily tugged me along with her because she probably assumed I would run. And honestly, I thought about it for like two point five seconds. It was pointless since everything I had was in the house I shared with my grandmother, but it sure was tempting. I wobble-limped alongside Sissily, glancing at my coven mates as they packed everything, including the Kishi demon I apprehended.

"She will chill out by the time we get back." My best friend gnawed on her lower lip, not believing her own assurances.

"I don't care." My shrug didn't fool her since I was patting my hair to smooth it and probably looked constipated just thinking about facing my grandmother behind closed doors.

Because Danika Byrnes never chilled. Like ever. My grandmother was born with a stick so far up her ass the goddess herself couldn't find it if she tried.

She was going to hand my ass to me, and I had no other choice but to take whatever she dished out. A sinking suspicion that it would involve cleaning churned in my stomach right beside the booze.

There was a first time for everything, though. She might've grown a heart in the last twelve hours. Or took it from some random jar and shoved it in her chest. My head tilted to the side, I contemplated it for a second.

One look at my grandmother's disappearing form, with

those stiff shoulders and that head held high, killed that hope. There was no escaping a punishment.

With a groan, I followed my best friend into the belly of the beast.

The whole way back to the coven, I kept trying to picture my eyeballs floating in a jar on top of my grandmother's desk.

They were a nice shade of golden honey, if I did say so myself. I'd have them in a jar too if I didn't need them.

Resting Witch Face: Chapter Two

The Gatekeeper's coven was located dab smack in the middle of Cleveland, of all places. The temple walls stretched high toward the sky like the open mouths of baby birds waiting for a worm to fall into their gaping maws. A domed ceiling made of glass, to better see the full moon each month, covered almost half the block. Made out of black stone, the building looked menacing, and the three keys – a symbol representing Hecate- painted in blood red above the tall double doors of the entrance stood out stark against it. Since it was late at night, magical flames were shooting seven feet tall on each side of the stars leading to it, casting it in an eerie-hellish hue. No wonder humans gave us a wide berth.

Pausing at the bottom of the marble steps that would lead me inside, I glanced up and down the street. An urge to book it down the sidewalk and find a place to hide for a day or two was very tempting. However, with only one boot and still mostly drunk, there was no way I could outrun Sissily. She might sympathize with me, but she was a stickler for the rules, and she was smart enough not to want to anger Danika, unlike me. I had no doubt she'd tackle me and drag me kicking and screaming inside by the hair. She did that once in middle school when I didn't want to go back inside with her after lunch break. The humans mulling around would be no help, either. Ever since we came out of the closet, so to speak, they gawked like we were circus freaks but wouldn't come closer than a few feet, as if magic was contagious and they might get infected. I wish it was.

There were exceptions like Davon the cop, but those were few and far between. We were "the others," and unless they needed help, humans wanted nothing to do with us. At least there were no pitchforks or burnings at the stake involved, so not bad I guessed. That was why my coven was very strict. The government told us we were all good to live among humans as long as no problems came up by *any* supernatural being, not just us. So, the high priest and my grandmother—to be honest it was probably all her because the priest was practically a mute when around her—decided we would boss the supernatural world around. The magi police force was just a front for posturing. We were the ones that got down and dirty. And destroyed perfectly new pairs of designer boots in the process, I'd like to add.

Sissily took my elbow and waddled me up the steps when I took too long to move. Chewing on the inside of my mouth, I allowed my fear to choke me until I reached the double doors, and then I squared my shoulders. Whatever issues I had would be left at the door. No one needed to know my shit. It was none of their business, anyway.

The inside of the building was also painted black, with a hallway like one long intestine twisting around offices, ritual rooms, guest reception halls, and the library, of course. Our pride and joy, with knowledge gathered for generation after generation by magical families. It was the largest collection in the world, and the love of my grandmother's life. I personally used it to hide from idiots when they got annoying, or to pretend I was busy when we had a ritual scheduled. If I was busy, I couldn't participate and see all the pitying looks or sneers thrown my way.

"You ready?" Sissily mumbled under her breath and dragged me out of my spinning thoughts.

"No."

"Hazel."

"Why does everyone think saying my name will help anything?" I jerked my elbow out of her pinching hold and tugged hard on the borrowed jacket to straighten it. My balance went sideways, and I pitched forward, but she tugged me back before I face planted. "Let me tell you, it does nothing but piss me off and feed my anxiety. I know what my name is. I've had it my whole life, thank you very much."

"You're stalling."

"No." I gasped dramatically. "What in the world gave you that idea?" Sissily rolled her blue peepers at me. "I really don't want to go in. I might puke all over her desk."

"You're so stupid." She snickered and bumped my shoulder. For her sake, my lips pulled to the side in a pathetic attempt at a smile.

With a sigh, I continued my impersonation of Quasimodo hobbling down the hall on one high-heeled boot and one bare foot, darting glances at the candelabras lining the walls. Black pillar candles burned in clusters with blue flames, the magical fire standing straight without a crackle or a flicker. They always looked like a painting that gave off light to me, and it didn't matter how many times I saw them.

"They are expecting you." We hadn't fully rounded the corner yet, but Mike made sure to shout it like he was playing bingo and just won. He leered at Sissily, but as soon as he met my glare, his head ducked down so fast he almost headbutted the desk.

"I see you didn't take your meds today, Mike?" I jabbed him conversationally, and Sissily snorted.

"What? Yes, I did." His face snapped up and reddened like a tomato. "Hey, I don't take medication."

I pursed my lips, eyeing him and pretending like I didn't believe him.

Something told me if I kept looking at him his head might explode. I was willing to test that theory, but I felt Danika's magic reaching, plus Sissily nudged me to get moving.

"Maybe you should." My suggestion to the creep in passing left him sneering. "Meds won't grow your brain, but it'll help with your complexion."

We left him stuttering and talking to himself about bitches and the goddess knew what other fairy tales he told himself. After he dared to treat my best friend like she was his personal punching bag while she dated him, I made it my business to mess him up every chance I had. I was pretty sure he cast a protection spell around himself specifically against me so I couldn't physically harm him. Good thing, too, because I didn't trust myself not to fillet him like a fish.

I flung the door open without a knock and hobble-hopped inside my grandmother's office with Sissily nipping on my heels. Stopping in my tracks, I took in the large, ornate-oak desk Danika Byrne sat ramrod straight behind. High Priest Shadowblood was behind her right shoulder, his face pinched so tight it looked like he was trying not to fart. His slicked dark hair, long, thin nose, and pointed chin brought the image of a crow perched on my grandmother's shoulder to my mind every time he did that, although I never dared mention it. But it wasn't those two that made me freeze with one foot in the air and one hand gripping the doorknob.

No, it was the third person in the room just to the left of Danika. In his late twenties to mid-thirties, he was a face I'd never seen before between these walls. His blond hair was shaved close to his skull on the sides, with the top left longer to drape over his forehead in a wave. Eyes the color of melted chocolate flicked my way when I opened the door, and they widened in interest—not enough to be obvious, but since I was staring at him like an idiot, I noticed. A square jaw and a nose with a slight bump at the bridge like it had been broken a time or two framed full lips more suitable to a woman than someone like him. Wide shoulders stretched his indigo button-down shirt, which was tucked into the waistband of dark slacks that emphasized his narrow waist and muscular body. I gawked for less than five seconds, but it was enough for one corner of his mouth to twitch. That little quirk snapped me out of my daze.

Spinning around, I bolted out of the office and plowed Sissily down. She would've fallen on her ass if I didn't catch her by the arm and drag her back out with me. The door closed behind us with a loud thump when I bodily carried her to the desk where Mike was still muttering curses at me.

"Give me your shoes." My best friend squeaked when I plopped her ass on the desk.

"What? Why?"

"Shoes woman. Now." My hand was wiggling in her face to show my urgency. "Questions later."

I yanked them off her feet myself because I had no time to explain why having shoes instead of one boot—regardless of how pretty said boot may look—was so important. Lifting her leg up pushed Sissily until she was leaning on her hands, and if I wasn't in a hurry I would've chortled at Mike's face. Poor schmuck almost swallowed his tongue when he received a face full of a ponytail, and his saucer-like eyes told me he didn't miss Sissily's boobs sticking up from her arched back. I even stabbed her foot in my one boot because I was a good friend like that, and then I was yanking her along with me to enter the office for the second time. She'd probably replace my shampoo with glue to pay me back for this, but I'd deal with it later.

When I stepped back inside the office, my grandmother arched an eyebrow not looking very pleased, which I ignored, of course. Being the nice little witch I was, I waited for Sissily to limp inside before I closed the door and guided her to the closest chair. Her blue eyes were spitting daggers at me the whole time. As Sissily dropped on the uncomfortable chair, I went as far as petting her head like a puppy that did potty, ignoring her glare the entire time. Then, I turned and beamed at everyone in the room, giving my grandmother a pointed look towards blondie that said help a girl out but I had a feeling my plea fell on deaf ears.

"Hazel, what happened tonight?" Danika Byrne got down to business, stapling her fingers under her chin and leaning her forearms heavily on the desk. If looks could kill, Sissily would be reading my obituary right now.

Smile frozen on my face to flash my pearly whites, I widened my eyes at her. "What?" My lips didn't move as I pushed the question through my teeth. My best friend groaned from the side.

"What in the goddess's name is wrong with you?" I swore lightning flashed in Danika's emerald eyes. "Are you hurt? Did the demon do anything to you?"

"We don't discuss coven business in front of strangers, Dani—I mean, Ma'am. Grandmother," I added that last bit lamely as an afterthought, and the thunderous expression twisting her features told me she didn't miss it.

"River Blackman is an apprentice of our high priest, Hazel." She looked down her nose at me like I was supposed to be psychic and guess who was who around here without introduction. "There are no strangers."

Wait, what?

"You can have your shoes back." With a groan, I turned to Sissily and started tugging the shoes off my feet. I shoved them in her face, and she recoiled as if I'd thrown snakes at her.

"I don't want them." She attempted to slap my hands away with a mortified look on her face, but I was very persistent when I needed to be.

"Well, you're having them." I jabbed them at her again. "Give me my boot."

"What in the world is going on?" We all ignored the high priest when he mumbled at no one in particular, sounding perplexed.

"You are aware that you are nuts, right?" Sissily muttered under her breath, but she tugged her shoes on, and I yanked the one boot over my foot.

"Of course. I'm an asshole, Sissily, but I'm not stupid." She blinked at my incredulous tone, but I was already turning toward the rest of the people in the room.

A muscle twitched under my grandmother's eye.

"When the call came for the demon, everyone that answered was at least twenty minutes away. Everyone in this room knows they are sneaky and fast." I figured I'd get it over with. "I was closest to the demon, so I answered the call and made sure he didn't escape. Long story short, he is in our hands and the warehouse ransacked ..." Danika's scowl was a creature all on its own. "I'm sure you don't want to hear my internal debate about sacrificing my new boots so he didn't get away, Grandmother."

Grating on my nerves was the fact that River's eyes were dancing with suppressed humor. *Laugh it up, asshole, because I'll make you cry soon enough.* I wasn't sure he read the message I shot his way through my narrowed gaze, but he couldn't say he wasn't warned. Being a dud was a sure thing to get you bullied in a coven full of powerful witches, so instead of dealing with that, I became a master at cracking their noses with my fist. The blondie wouldn't know what hit him.

"I do want to hear every detail there is. Starting with what possessed you to go there in the first place. Fighting a demon without magic is unacceptable." If she noticed my flinch, she didn't show it. "He could've killed the last of the Byrne line, you insolent girl."

"How's this for a recap, Danika?" I snarled. The gasp from Shadowblood sounded scandalized when I slapped both hands on her desk and leaned forward so we were at eye level. "I can kick any demon's ass, including every idiot you have inside this coven, in six-inch heels, without breaking a sweat, and with my arms tied behind my back. I showed up at the warehouse, cracked the demon's head on the concrete like a melon, then I stabbed him with my new boot. Which you owe me a new pair, plus an iPhone, just so you know. Then the rest of you waltzed into posture with your magic and clean up the place. That good enough of an explanation for you?"

"How dare you speak like that?" High Priest Shadowblood stuttered, his neck elongating as he tucked his chin in. "You are not a savage, young lady."

"Aren't I, though?"

"Show respect to your grandmother," he snapped.

"You got one thing right, pops." My empty stare flicked his way, and he took an involuntary step back. If they don't string me from the roof tonight, I'm honestly never drinking again. "*My* grandmother, and I'm doing exactly what she taught me. To quote her, 'you treat people the way they treat you.' So, I will talk to her however damn well I please. In this case, I'm showing her the same respect she gave me." I believe Shadowblood was about to have an aneurism.

"Hazel," Danika leaned back in her chair on a sigh, all fight draining out of her. "I wasn't trying to insult you because you have no magic."

For an old witch, barely any lines were visible on her beautiful face. She might be a stick-up-the-ass nag, but no one could dispute the fact she still turned heads. Midnight blue hair spilled around her face like a waterfall, bringing attention to her alabaster skin and piercing emerald eyes. Tall for a woman, she was curvy where it counted, but most admirable of all was her presence. When Danika Byrne walked into a room, you knew it even if your back was turned.

"No, you were complimenting me on a job well done." With one last stare at Shadowblood, I pushed off the desk. "If we are done here, I need a shower. I can smell the Kishi demon on my skin."

"I need you to promise me—"

"I will not step foot anywhere where your precious witches with magic need to go." My smile could cut glass when I looked at her over my shoulder. "I'll just stand back and look pretty."

"You are not replaceable, Miss Byrne—" Shadowblood started, but I cut him off.

"No, I'm to be kept as a broodmare, High Priest Shadowblood. I'm aware." That got the reaction I expected from my grandmother.

"For the next week, you will be cleaning the library, Hazel," Danika snapped and stood to her full height, which was a couple of inches higher than mine. She did it on purpose so I had to look up at her. *Nice power play, Grandma.* "And the ritual room, too, until I say that you are done. Am I clear?"

"Crystal." I dared a glance at River, but with his hands clasped at the small of his back, he was frowning at his boots. *Welcome to the Gatekeeper's Coven, blondie, this is how we treat family.* The guy hasn't done anything to me, but just seeing him standing behind that desk with Danika and Shadowblood put him in my shit bucket, too.

"Let's go," I called out to my best friend, who was in the office for moral support more than anything else.

We almost made it out the door. Almost.

"Sissily, you'll join Hazel in her tasks." My grandmother was already back in her chair and had turned to say something to River Blackman, a blunt dismissal of us if ever I saw one.

We spilled out of the office without another word. "Why do I pay every time you get into trouble, little jerk?"

"Because you are the only one that can call me that and live, big jerk." I threaded my arm through hers, leaning against her for support.

"True." She sighed and placed her head on my shoulder. "On a good note, not even you can get in trouble inside a library."

Lesson 2: *never tempt fate.*

That bitch bit.

Resting Witch Face: Chapter Three

"Hazel?"

Sissily's tone was low when she hissed my name, but in the silence of the library, it boomed like a gun going off next to my ear. My head jerked up for no reason at all since I knew she'd be coming to join me. The back of my skull connected with the thick wooden shelf above me with a dull heavy thud, which made dark roses bloom at the corners of my eyes as I crawled backward, extracting myself from my hidey hole. I had no doubt my best friend had a perfect view of my ass sticking up in the air while I wiggled my way out, but my glare made sure any comment she had stayed behind her closed mouth.

Her lips stayed pressed closed for exactly thirty seconds. Tops.

"I still don't understand why you had to take my shoes," Sissily grumbled under her breath, still stuck on the same thing two days later as she handed me a stack of ancient texts we had to catalogue. Courtesy of the Kishi demon I nailed with my poor ankle boot.

"That should be your answer." Her elbow connected with my side, forcing me to grunt. Exasperated, I huffed, shaking the books in my hands at her face. "You can't understand why you would need to leave a good first impression because you have magic, woman. That's all a guy in our world needs to feel and he gets the googly eyes. I, on the other hand, don't have magic. Apart from the respect I receive around here ..."

"That's not respect, Hazel. They're afraid of you. There is a difference," she told me so calmly you'd think she just gave me a compliment.

"That's beside the point. As I was saying, I only have the respect, so I have to make a good impression with my sense of style, too." We both knew I was talking smack. If I stopped doing that, I would have to curl up in a ball and start rocking back and forth.

"I still don't get the shoes."

"Hecate help me, would you stop with the damned shoes? I didn't want to limp on one boot like a dumbass in front of a hottie, okay? How was I to know blondie was one of Grandmother's pawns?" Admitting my vanity was never easy, although she knew me better than I knew myself.

"He is easy on the eyes, I'll give you that." A smile ghosted her mouth, and she bumped me with her shoulder while tucking a loose strand of hair behind her ear.

"Great. Have at it because he is all yours. In the meantime, grab that stack of books over there." Pointing my chin at the pile ready to tip over, I pushed the last book in my hands on the shelf between two others.

In a normal life, when someone told you that you'd be cleaning a library, you'd expect rows of books lining the walls and pretty tables with single little lamps where people could read in peace and quiet. Since nothing was as it should be in this place, half of the vast room was packed with jars full of floating eyeballs, teeth, fingers, or other body parts I tried very hard not to pay too close attention to. A shiver raked my spine, and my friend noticed.

"Ignore those, I'll fix them up." Sissily allowed me to keep my dignity because we both knew I'd end up begging her to do it so I didn't have to touch them. "I honestly don't know why you insist that everyone thinks you are this mean little shit when you have a heart of gold." She shuffled back to me with an armful of tomes, not missing my grimace. "You can say whatever you want, but I know you."

"I should kill you so you keep my secret, then." I snatched the books, turning my back so she didn't see the tears that prickled the back of my eyes.

"Do try, I'm begging you," my friend purred, cocking her hip.

Sissily was the strongest witch in our coven after Danika and Shadowblood. She had every right to be cocky, and for the life of me, up to this day, I couldn't tell why she chose me to be best friends with. By doing that, she made sure her name was whispered behind our backs by all the petty witches in our community, too. A fact that rubbed me wrong on so many levels and made me bare my teeth at everyone, while she couldn't care less about the gossip mill. Regardless of what she said, it was her with the heart of gold, taking strays—or duds as it was in my case—under her protection. Coven mates tried using their magic against me at the beginning, knowing I couldn't fight back the same way, until she unleashed ropes of fire and sent a few of them to the infirmary with third-degree burns. Danika was ready to peel the skin off her bones until she walked in and saw us with arms wrapped around each other, jutting our chins at her in defiance. After a long, loaded look, my grandmother's mouth twitched at the edges and she walked away without a word. We were four at the time, and since that day, we'd been glued at the hip. Unfortunately for my friend, that meant she got in a lot of trouble because of me. I had no magic, but I had fists.

"Do I look dumb to you?" I pointed at myself. "I didn't think so."

Sissily giggled and walked to the floor-to-ceiling shelves full of jars across from where I was standing. "How much longer do you think she will hold us here?" In jeans, a t-shirt, and with her hair in a ponytail, she looked comfy, unlike me in my skirt and blouse.

"I don't know," I answered honestly with a sigh. "If I kept my mouth shut, we may have gone without punishment, but I just couldn't let that go. I swear sometimes I think Danika says things on purpose because she knows I'll react. If I didn't know better, I'd say she rubs salt in an open wound when she needs both of us out of her way."

"What do you mean?" Sissily twisted toward me, hugging a jar full of imp fingers to her chest.

I sawed my teeth over my lower lip, contemplating if I should voice my thoughts or keep my mouth shut. When her blue eyes narrowed on me, I knew I better speak up or she'd never let it go. My best friend was as stubborn as a mule.

"She knows that not having magic is a sore subject for me." Eyes darting around to make sure no one was around, I took a couple of steps closer to her, keeping my tone low. "It's a sore subject for her, too, since I've heard her raging about idiots and how they didn't value their lives because they treated me like I was nothing. So why else would she slap my lack of magic in my face unless she wanted me punished and out of her way?"

I could almost hear the gears turning in Sissily's head. The corners of her mouth slanted slightly down, and the edges of her eyes narrowed. She had her thinking face on while her eyes searched mine.

"Every time I'm punished, you are in the same boat, too ..." I trailed off.

"In the last seven to eight months, more so than ever." Sissily nodded, the jars completely forgotten.

"Well, now that you mention it, yeah." Frowning, I ignored the unease swirling inside me. Witches came to their full potential of power at the age of twenty-three, which for both of us was a few years ago. My best friend and I had our birthdays three days apart, and we were both twenty-six now, so that couldn't be the reason for Danika tucking us away more often than usual. "I can't think of a reason—"

"I can." Plonking the jar with a loud thump, Sissily snatched my hand and dragged me deeper between the rows of books. "About nine months ago, the other covens called a meeting in Atlanta. Do you remember?" She waited for my head to dip in confirmation before continuing. "According to Mike—"

"You still talk to that douchebag?" My mouth closed shut with a snap when she shot me a glare.

"The other covens pressured Danika to reassess the contributions of her coven because it's not fair"—She used air quotes and twisted her mouth— "for most of the Gatekeeper's Coven to be in power. Apparently, they had witches in their ranks, which would be a better fit for enforcers. I think the new guy is here for that reason, by the way."

"And I jumped in to apprehend a Kishi demon with no magic at all." With a groan, I buried my face in both hands, ignoring the comment about River.

"Yeah." Her nails dug into my forearm where she was still holding onto me. "So, if what you have noticed is true, I will bet my magic it has something to do with that."

"There you are, Hazel." The words died on my tongue, and I spun around to face the witch smirking at us from the other end of the shelves. I wanted to tell Sissily what I said was only a suspicion gnawing at me and not facts, but it'd have to wait.

"Is there a reason you are breathing the same air as me?" I asked Sasha Airborne, nemesis number one from our coven. Sissily clutching my arm made it look like she was holding me so I didn't jump the witch, which worked in my favor.

She took a step back before catching herself.

"The crescent moon chamber needs to be cleaned for the midnight ritual." Her drawled words made me grind my teeth, and Sissily clamped her fingers harder on my forearm. "The High Priest Shadowblood said you need to do it stat. So chop-chop, get to it."

"Hazel ..." Sissily hissed, but I shook her off and was already striding to Sasha.

The witch didn't have time to bolt before I stood in front of her and grabbed a fistful of her shirt, twisting it in my grip to bring us nose to nose. She could've been beautiful with her flame-red hair and sky-blue eyes, if she wasn't a snake.

"Last time I checked, Shadowblood is perfectly capable of speaking for himself. Why are you here?" My crazy eyes reflected back at me in her wide-eyed gaze. This close, I'd knock her ass out before she had time to call on her magic, and we both knew it.

Grab your copy…
vinci-books.com/restingwitch

About the Author

Maya Daniels, USA Today Bestselling and multi-award-winning supernatural suspense author, is a fun-loving woman with many talents.

She traveled the world, gaining life experiences that helped her career as an investigative journalist, as well as her storytelling. Maya writes compelling tales of magic, mythical creatures, loyalty, and life-changing friendships with snarky female characters—much like herself.

Her travels have taken her to Europe, Africa, Asia, Australia, and America. Born with her feet in motion, she currently resides in Ohio, spinning her next epic story that you will not want to put down.

Her biggest 'sins' are her love of chocolate and coffee—through an IV drip! One to never sit still, Maya practices Reiki healing, different types of martial arts, reads about the arcane, talks to furry creatures more than humans, picks up a sledgehammer for home improvement, and travels with her fated mate, seeking her own adventures.

www.ingramcontent.com/pod-product-compliance
Ingram Content Group UK Ltd.
Pitfield, Milton Keynes, MK11 3LW, UK
UKHW040036130426
469799UK00003B/124